To Mark and Danielle —
superheroes, super friends.
— L.L.

Scholastic Canada Ltd.
604 King Street West, Toronto, Ontario M5V 1E1, Canada

Scholastic Inc.
557 Broadway, New York, NY 10012, USA

Scholastic Australia Pty Limited
PO Box 579, Gosford, NSW 2250, Australia

Scholastic New Zealand Limited
Private Bag 94407, Botany, Manukau 2163, New Zealand

Scholastic Children's Books
Euston House, 24 Eversholt Street, London NW1 1DB, UK

www.scholastic.ca

Library and Archives Canada Cataloguing in Publication

Livingston, Lesley, author
      Super sketchy / Lesley Livingston ; illustrated by Britt Wilson.

(The almost epic squad)
Issued in print and electronic formats.
ISBN 978-1-4431-5785-8 (hardcover).--ISBN 978-1-4431-5786-5 (ebook)

      I. Wilson, Britt, 1986-, illustrator II. Title.

PS8623.I925S87 2019   jC813'.6   C2018-905889-7
                                                          C2018-905890-0

Illustrations and hand lettering by Britt Wilson.
Cover background image copyright © Piotrurakau/Getty Images.

6 5 4 3 2 1   Printed in Canada 114   19 20 21 22 23

MIX
Paper from
responsible sources
FSC® C016245

DIMLY, MANITOBA. THIRTEEN YEARS AGO.

SHHH . . . STILL FAST ASLEEP. THE STORM'S NOT BOTHERING THE NEWBORNS.

zzzt

FFZZt

EMERGENCY SYSTEM

THE EMERGENCY LIGHTING SYSTEM OVERLOADS!

Z-ZZ KSSHH FSS

A CLOUD OF GLOWING DUST RAINS DOWN ONTO THE SLEEPING BABIES.

BEEP BEEP BEE

BABY FLEM GETS A NOSEFUL.

BABY LUNDBORG IS SPRINKLED DOWN THE SPINE.

THE RIGHT SIDE OF BABY KILDARE'S CRANIUM IS DUSTED.

BABY O'KAYE SWALLOWS A MOUTHFUL.

2

DR. FASSBINDER! THE LIGHTS . . . DUST . . . THE BABIES! THEY'RE GLOWING!

GLOWING, NURSE NUSSBAUM?

YESSSS! IT'S THE CHANCE OF A LIFETIME!

WHA . . . ?!

THEY'VE BEEN IR-REID-IATED!

REIDIUM (ATOMIC NUMBER $13\frac{1}{2}$): AN INCREDIBLY RARE AND VOLATILE ELEMENT. WHEN REFINED WITH GARLIC, IT HAS HUGE ENERGY POTENTIAL. BUT AFTER SEVERAL DISASTERS, INDUSTRIES DEEMED IT TOO DANGEROUS. SOME REIDIUM REMAINS, IN THE REMOTE MOUNTAINS OF PIANVIA AND HERE IN SLEEPY DIMLY.

DIMLY BULB LIGHTING & TULIPS

THESE BABIES COULD CHANGE THE WORLD!

THE HOSPITAL STILL USES DIMLY REIDIUM BULBS! I'VE DONE REIDIUM EXPERIMENTS ON RODENTS.

AND . . .

MEET MY LAB ASSISTANTS.

THIS IS STAN. AND THERE'S DAPHNE, CLAUDE, ELAINE, AL . . . AND GERALD.

UH. HELLO?

DIMLY GEN

LET'S GET HOME AND CELEBRATE WITH MEAT LOAF!

4

THEIR SPECIAL POWERS MAY NOT SHOW UNTIL PUBERTY. THAT'S HOW IT WAS WITH THE MICE. BUT THEN THEY'LL BE EPIC!

TILL THEN THEY'RE ... WELL ... ALMOST EPIC!

FASSBINDER AND NUSSBAUM PRESS ON AS A TEAM. MORE THAN ONE KIND OF SPARK FLIES.

BUT LOVE DOESN'T KEEP YOU IN GARLIC. DESPERATE FOR FUNDING, FASSBINDER CONTACTS SECRET GOVERNMENT DEPARTMENT C, IN CHARGE OF PROBLEMS NO ONE ELSE TAKES SERIOUSLY.

FUTURE SUPERPOWERS ARE LIKELY!

FROM: DEPARTMENT C TO: DR. FASSBINDER SUBJECT: FUNDING (NOT MUCH) APPROVED.

FINALLY, AFTER ALL THESE YEARS. A CHANCE TO PROVE ...

I MUST GO. THE WORK IS IMPORTANT.

THERE'S ONLY FUNDING FOR ONE.

BUT WHAT ABOUT US?

CAST ASIDE, NURSE NUSSBAUM GOES ROGUE AND SEEKS POWER FOR HERSELF.

TEN POUNDS OF GARLIC.

A HALF OUNCE OF REIDIUM . . .

KA-BOOM

NOTHING REMAINS BUT THE STENCH OF SCORCHED RUBBER-SOLED NURSING SHOES.

OR SO IT SEEMS . . .

DR. FASSBINDER AND HIS ASSISTANTS CONTINUE THEIR EXPERIMENTS IN A TOP-SECRET LAB IN MONTREAL, TESTING THE CHILDREN FOR "GIFTED" EVERY YEAR . . .

MEANWHILE, SOMEONE KNOWN ONLY AS "THE BOSS" QUIETLY RECRUITS A TEAM OF NEFARIOUS MINIONS TO SHADOW THE ALMOST EPIC KIDS . . .

. . . AND TAKES TO THE SKIES IN A TATTERED BLIMP. EVER ANGRY, EVER EVIL, EVER SMELLING OF BURNT RUBBER, AND IMPATIENTLY AWAITING THE CHILDREN AND THEIR POWERS.

BUT WHAT OF THE CHILDREN TODAY?

7

CHAPTER 1

ARTSY-SMARTSY . . .

Destiny struck Daisy Kildare like a bolt of lightning on the morning of her thirteenth birthday. The second her eyes popped open, she dove for a stack of glossy brochures piled neatly on her dressing table.

"Art!" Daisy proclaimed. "Art is my true calling. Or, at least, it will be. I mean . . . how hard could it be?"

She fanned out the pamphlets — plucked from the table outside the guidance office the week before — on her floral bedspread, like a deck of cards. Since moving halfway across the country with her mom and starting at Pendrell Public School in West Vancouver, Daisy had been made aware, in no uncertain terms, that May Long Weekend Activity Camps were a Thing in her new school.

Even the banner above the table where the brochures were stacked had read: *CHOOSE YOUR CAMP . . . SEIZE YOUR DESTINY!!*

Yup. *Two* exclamation marks.

The prospect had been intimidating at first. Daisy had never been to any kind of camp back in her hometown — Dimly, Manitoba — and she wasn't up on all the campy protocols. Like, how did a person even figure out which one to go to, for starters? There were hundreds of the things! Well, dozens, maybe. The whole thing had made Daisy feel left out whenever camp chatter broke out in the halls between classes.

And now the selection deadlines were fast approaching. "Archery Camp, Fashion Camp, Great British Columbia Bake-Off Camp . . ." she muttered, shuffling the flyers. "Guitar Camp. Drama Camp. Yoga Camp. Yogourt Camp . . ." (*Vancouver sure is weird*, she thought) ". . . X-Treme Jazz Camp. Jazzy X-Treme Camp. Math Camp. Skateboard Camp. Code Camp. Parkour Camp. Rock-Climbing Camp. Camping Camp . . ."

Two of the pamphlets were stuck together. Daisy peeled away the Cooking with Kale Camp brochure and — *there*! Finally. The one she'd been searching for.

"Art Camp!" she exclaimed triumphantly.

She swept the rest of the pamphlets off the bed and into the wastebasket and, feeling optimistic about Camp Week for the very first time, went about the business of getting ready for school.

"Destiny," she muttered, gripping the Art Camp brochure between her teeth as she tugged on a pair of overalls over a sunflower T-shirt. She topped it all off with a floppy felt hat. She'd probably fit right in at Art Camp. Right?

The funny thing was, it remained a mystery as to what, exactly, had prompted Daisy to go down *that* particular path on *that* particular morning. Maybe it was the birthday vibe. But if you were to ask her, she'd probably have just blinked at you in confusion.

The initial spark of motivation was already lost by the time she'd brushed her teeth and run a comb through her wavy brown hair.

Never mind. Her fingertips were itching to pick up a pencil. *Tingling* a little, even . . . And if she'd been in less of a rush to make it to school on time, she might have noticed that one small detail.

CHAPTER 2

ARTFULLY DODGED

"Seriously?" Daisy muttered as she sat on the hall floor, back pressed against her locker. She glared at the pencil held tightly in her grasp. "I seem to recall asking 'how hard could it be?' earlier today, but I meant that as a rhetorical question."

It wasn't until lunchtime that she'd even had a chance to dig her pencil case out of her knapsack. But in the few precious moments before the next bell, she was determined to take her new-found Destiny out for a test doodle. With, so far, limited success.

She thought she'd start with something simple, having read somewhere that some old painter dude back in the old days had made a name for himself with pictures of sunflowers. Again, how hard could it be? Daisy hummed to herself as she dug through her supplies, ripped a sheet of blank paper from the back of a notebook, and chose a freshly sharpened coloured pencil aptly named "Sunflower Yellow."

"Okay . . . here we go!"

She attacked the page with gusto. But after three or four minutes of intense scribbling, the yellow lead in the coloured pencil snapped and the image left behind more closely resembled a stubborn mustard stain than any cheerful bloom.

"Huh."

Okaay . . . maybe something a little less . . . robust, she thought. *A tree, say.*

Daisy fished out a green pencil. The lead didn't snap this time, but it *did* wear down to a blunt nub pretty quickly, with nothing but a page of non-tree-shaped blotches to show for it. Daisy crumpled the page and shoved it into the depths of her knapsack.

"Hrmph."

Okaaay . . . maybe diving into colour right off the bat was ambitious. Or perhaps she just wasn't properly inspired. Or maybe flora wasn't her forte. Daisy tapped the coloured pencil against her teeth, lost in thought for a moment as the other students of Pendrell Public streamed past her in the hall. She glanced down at the candy-confettied birthday cupcake her mom had left her that morning, carefully packed in a zipper baggie and tied with a bow. And she was struck by an idea. Inspiration!

It wasn't just *her* birthday that day. It was also her best friend's birthday. But she was on the other side of the country, almost. Jessica Flem was still happily hunkered down in Dimly, a scruffy little burg in — as far as Daisy had always figured — almost exactly the middle of nowhere. Up until she'd actually had to leave it, Daisy couldn't wait to get out of there.

Daisy reached in her bag and fished out the card she'd picked up a few days earlier. A best friend was the best sort of inspiration. To go along with the brief wave of homesickness that washed over her in that moment, Daisy chose a regular-looking grey-leaded pencil. She'd taken it from a box of Dimly Bulb Co. promotional pencils her mom had brought home from work before the two of them had packed up and moved.

You'd think Daisy would have noticed the *tingling* in her fingers again . . .

But, no. Instead, she signed the card and wrote Happy Birthday, with a quick note about how she missed hanging out, how Vancouver was weird and how her mom still wouldn't let her have a real cellphone for "reasons" and so she was stuck with one of those ancient flippy things that could barely even text. Daisy couldn't even pretend it was retro cool, like her wardrobe choices.

She thought about adding another sentence letting Jess know she'd decided on a Destiny, but instead she let her artistic genius speak for itself and tried her hand at sketching a self-portrait on the card.

Concentrating fiercely, Daisy gripped the Dimly pencil hard enough to turn her knuckles pale and stuck her tongue out of the corner of her mouth. Her eyebrows knit together. The pencil tip hovered over the surface of the card as she conjured a mental picture of her own smiling features.

Suddenly, Daisy felt not just a *tingling* but a powerful electric jolt sizzling from her fingertips all the way up into the centre of her skull — like a *ZzAApp!* of lightning. Her drawing hand skittered and fluttered, zigzagging across the page seemingly all on its own, for a frantic flurry of seconds.

Aaaand . . . *done!*

"Voila! Art!" she exclaimed as she opened her eyes to peer at her masterpiece. "Er . . ."

She turned the birthday card this way and that, trying to make heads or, well, heads out of it. In depicting her mildly wavy hair, Daisy's drawing had taken on a frenzied aspect, corkscrews sproinging out from her head in every direction.

As for her face, well, you couldn't tell much of the detail behind the hair-splosion. Staring at her baffling self-portrait, Daisy didn't notice the bell signalling the end of lunch or her fellow students on their reluctant stampede back to class. She *did* notice when one of them tripped over her outstretched legs, sprawling like a gangly starfish in the middle of the busy corridor. A burst of laughter bounced off the lockers.

"Maybe watch where you're going?" Daisy muttered, before realizing that she knew the boy.

Where do I know that kid from? she thought, considering she hadn't really known anyone at Pendrell long enough to remember them. And then it came to her: *Oh yeah. Archie O'Kaye. Huh.*

Daisy had known Archie O'Kaye as long as she'd known Jess. Which is to say, all her life. Archie was also from Dimly, and the three of them — along with a kinda doofus-y kid named Gary Lundborg — had been maternity-ward roommates in their first few days on the planet. Jess and Daisy had gone on to become fast friends; Gary and Jess had developed a fierce online gaming rivalry; and Archie . . . Well, Archie had been, uh, *there?* Up until a few years back, at least, when he had moved away from Dimly. Daisy had pretty much forgotten all about him.

To be entirely truthful, even though she'd vaguely recognized him in assembly on her first day at Pendrell, Daisy hadn't been able to recall much about him from an outstanding-personality-traits point of view. Back in Dimly, he'd just been Archie. They'd shared a brief, awkward reunion that first day and then made a point of avoiding each other.

Daisy shook her head. How had she managed to wind up living in the same place — and going to the same school — as one of her old nursery mates from Dimly General?

But, here she was. And now here *he* was, sprawled face down in the middle of the hallway in front of fifty pointing-laughing-heckling students. She felt a little bad for him.

Gah . . . She cringed on his behalf when she thought she saw something that might, for just a fleeting second, have been fear or embarrassment in Archie's eyes . . . But then he leaped to his feet, Jess Flem's birthday card in his hand.

"Good heavens!" Archie exclaimed, waving a hand over her doodle like a magician doing a card trick. "I was distracted by this . . . gosh . . . this *masterpiece!* Yes. I think that's the, uh, *right* word"

"Uh?" Daisy blinked at him, puzzled.

Masterpiece? Is he being sarcastic?

"It's genius!" The word rolled off Archie's tongue like buttered silk. Which was a weird metaphor for Daisy to wrap her head around, but that's *exactly* what his voice sounded like. Smooth and whispery, luxurious and liquidy all at once.

He could've called her self-portrait a third-rate juice cup stain and she wouldn't have cared. Daisy just wanted to stand there and listen to him talk.

She wasn't the only one. The whole hallway had screeched to a sudden, silent standstill. The entire Pendrell student body, it seemed, was leaning forward, slack-jawed, in anticipation of what Archie O'Kaye would say next.

"My dear girl," he continued in the dulcet tones of a high-society art critic, "this is a masterpiece to rival the, well, the masters' pieces. You know, the paintings by all those dead guys with the funny names?"

Is he . . . mocking me? Daisy wondered again for a brief moment.

"They couldn't touch you with a ten-foot paintbrush." He put his fingertips to his lips and made a kissing noise. "Magnifique!"

Is he . . . serious?

As Archie continued to sing her artistic praises, Daisy found herself compelled to believe him. Students on either side had drifted close, craning their necks and peering over each other's shoulders to try to catch a glimpse of the masterpiece he described. His words held a hypnotic sway over anyone in earshot.

And it wasn't just students. Mrs. Winklehorn, the art teacher, suddenly screeched to a halt near the library double doors and did an about-face.

Daisy couldn't help but notice that Mrs. W.'s ears were practically swivelling side to side on her head, like radar dishes seeking the source of a transmission. Her eyes bulged from their sockets behind oversized mauve-tinted glasses the instant they latched on to the card in Archie's hand.

"What is this?" she asked. "What-what-what?" She sounded like a chicken as she shuffled and elbowed her way through the crowd of students, making grabby hands for the sketch.

"It's geeEEeeniusss," Archie said again, his voice swooping and diving, echoing off the lockers and wrapping everyone in a warm vocal hug.

"So it *is*," the art teacher murmured, turning the card this way and that, as if trying to make sense of the image in spite of her words.

"It's . . . it's . . . well, let's just call it a . . . um, a . . ." Her eyes went small and beady behind her glasses as she peered at the thing. ". . . an abstract-Impressionist-absurdist gem. A Pollock. A Picasso. Cézanne, Seurat, Gauguin, van Gogh . . ."

"Right!" Archie nodded enthusiastically, persuasively. "The funny-name guys." He turned to a bedazzled Daisy. "See?"

"Yes!" The art teacher was almost swooning. "Archie, you are so very right. I must know who is responsible! Who-who-who?"

From chicken to owl, thought Daisy.

"Is it you, Dale?" She turned to the girl at Archie's elbow. But Dale wasn't paying attention. Her eyes were half closed, like she was meditating. Or maybe she had a stomach ache.

"Uday?" She turned to the boy standing behind Dale. Uday shook his head, mesmerized alternately by the doodle and Dale.

"No, no," Archie said. "It was none other than the delightful Delilah Kilburn—"

"Daisy Kildare—"

"Daisy Kil*dare*, yes that's it," he said, gliding over the name bobble so smoothly Daisy wasn't even sure it had happened. "A bright light from my very own charming hometown of Dimly, Manitoba." He said it with a wink, a grin and a sweeping hand gesture — like Daisy was a contestant in a pageant.

"Delightful . . . yes . . ." the art teacher murmured. Then she seemed to snap out of it and her mauve-tinted gaze locked on to Daisy's face like the laser-sights of a submarine torpedo launcher. "YOU." She pointed a mauve-painted nail at Daisy's nose. "*You* will attend my Art Camp in the coming break. *We* will foster your creative magnificence. *I* will make the arrangements. *It* is your *Destiny.*"

"Um, well, yeah," Daisy shrugged in helpless bemusement. "That's kinda what *I* thought, but . . ." She frowned at the card Archie still held. "But . . ."

But nothing, apparently. The matter was decided. In a flurry of scarves, Mrs. Winklehorn spun and headed off in the direction of the school office.

Archie stopped talking. The rest of the students shook themselves like puppies waking from naps. And Daisy stood there, baffled by what had just happened.

She blinked at Archie, then snatched her sketch from his hand.

He blinked back at her. Then he snorted. "Wow! Call that art?" he said. "I've got a shirt with spaghetti stains that show more talent."

And Archie turned and disappeared down the

hall before Daisy could kick him in the shin. *What a weirdo*, she thought, stung by the switcheroo art critique. Maybe her sketch wasn't exactly suitable for framing, but he didn't have to make fun of it. Neither, for that matter, did the art teacher. Because, *clearly*, that's what had just happened . . . wasn't it?

Destiny. Hrmph.

The crowd of students thinned and drifted away. Daisy stooped and shoved everything — pencils, paper, floppy hat — into her knapsack. She was already late for her next class and a visit to the principal's office was a different kind of Destiny than the one she'd been aiming for.

But if she'd only turned to catch a glimpse of her reflection as she ran past the glass trophy case in the school's main vestibule, she might have realized that there was definitely something different about her that day.

CHAPTER 3

CLUMSY-DUMBSY . . . !

Kip Winklehorn took a deep breath. Then he tossed his head to flip the hair out of his face, rubbed his sweaty palms on the legs of his jeans, and picked his target: a ledge on the far side of the stairwell that led to the school basement. Easy enough — the jump across the well was only about a metre and there was a drainpipe to catch onto once he was on the other side. And then the fire-escape ladder . . .

Kip bounced on the balls of his feet, then launched into a slow, loping run. "Leaf on the wind, Kipper," he whispered as he ran. "Leafonthe . . . wiiiiii— YIKES!"

Kip hadn't accounted for the rain. Which, considering he lived in *Vancouver*, was something of a GLARING oversight. Granted, it was sunny at the time of his leap, but it had been raining only moments earlier. The slick pavement made the soles of his sneakers slip. Which made his legs kick up.

And the "leaf on the wind" did a mid-air double barrel roll that would have netted Kip a lot of likes on the FacePlant channel under the category of "OOOH, That's Gonna Leave a Mark." Too bad Kip could never convince any of his friends with camera phones to join him in his parkour exploits. Or, maybe not. It had probably been pretty embarrassing. It had *certainly* been painful. And Kip didn't really have that many friends to speak of anyway.

He lay sprawled at the bottom of the stairs, a wiry tangle of arms and legs, contemplating another attempt. It was a good thing Kip had dragged an old gym mat down the stairwell to cushion the concrete steps. Not that the padding had done anything to keep his head from connecting enthusiastically with the green steel door at the tail end of his tumble.

"Ow." He rubbed at the goose egg he could already feel rising up under his thatch of brown hair.

"Dude."

Kip looked up to see the shadowed silhouette of a floppy-hat-wearing girl peering down at him.

"Are you okay?"

"Yeah. Yup. Good." Kip grunted as he pushed

himself up to his hands and knees, and then up to standing — a little wobbly — at the bottom of the stairs. "Totally fine . . ."

"What the heck were you trying to prove just now?" she asked.

Kip saw that the face beneath the floppy hat belonged to the new kid at school. *What was her name? Daffodil, maybe?*

"Daisy Kildare," she said, extending a hand to help him as he clambered up from the depths of the stairwell. "New-ish kid at school."

"Kip Winklehorn," he answered. "Uh . . . Black 'n' blue-ish kid at school."

"You, like, some kinda ninja? Uh . . . in training?"

"Heh." Kip brushed at the dirt scuff on his jeans and T-shirt. "I wish. I'm just practising for my entrance tryout for Parkour Camp this weekend."

"Wait." Daisy blinked at him. "Out of all the camps — and *wow* there are a *lot* of them — *that's* the one you chose?"

"It chose me. Parkour is a calling."

A sudden breeze caught Daisy's hat and lifted it into the air. She made a grab for it, but it tumbled out of reach.

"I'll get it!" Kip exclaimed, launching himself into the same loping run he used to start a parkour sequence. There was a tree to the left, and Kip jumped, aiming for a low branch — which he *actually* managed to land on — before propelling himself, hands outstretched, into the air. But just then the wind died to utter stillness. The hat dropped gracefully, right through his hands, like an octopus flopping down to the sea bottom.

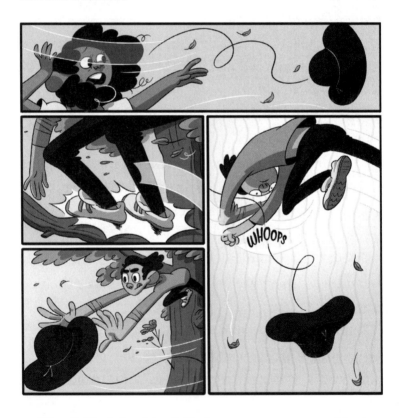

Kip flailed in his failed rescue attempt. Having overshot his mark, he dropped — rather less gracefully than the hat — to the ground, where he tumbled straight into a thorny hedge.

"Ow."

"Your 'calling,' huh?" Daisy raised an eyebrow and retrieved her headwear.

"Yeah." Kip sighed. "Too bad I keep dialing the wrong number."

He disentangled himself from the hedge, and he and Daisy jogged over to wait out another cloudburst beneath a tree as the sky opened up and soaked the schoolyard. Daisy tugged her hat on over a wild tangle of sproingy hair. She frowned in confusion when the hat popped back off, muttered something about West Coast humidity, and tried again, jamming the thing firmly onto her noggin.

"You get used to it," Kip said, trying to avoid staring as she wrangled the headgear down over the bird's nest of squiggly strands. "Where are you from, anyway?"

"No place *you'd* know," Daisy snorted.

"Oh," Kip said. "Well, excuse me for asking."

"No!" Daisy realized how that had sounded and hastened to explain. "I actually mean that. It's no place *anyone* would know! I mean, anyone normal. It's, like, Nowheresville. A mistake on a map. The kind of place a malfunctioning GPS wouldn't even accidentally send you to."

Kip blinked at her. "Okay . . . has it got a name?"

"*Pff.* Yeah. Appropriately enough: Dimly." She rolled her eyes. "Dimly—"

"Dimly, Manitoba!" Kip exclaimed. "I know all about it! Dimly Bulbs, Dimly graphite and Dimly Splotnik."

Daisy stared at Kip, her jaw drifting open in astonishment. "You're freaking me out," she said. "How do you know about those things?"

"My mom is the art teacher at Pendrell," Kip said. "Like my grandma was before her—"

"Wait. Your mom *inherited* a teaching position?"

"Ha. Yeah, I guess so." He shrugged. "Anyway, those three things are — or were — the holy trinity of art supplies for a whole artistic movement way back in the seventies. At least, that's what Gram always says. Dimly Bulbs are, like, super incandescent. The reidium filaments glow with a light that artists love. And Dimly graphite is *the* best for sketching.

"As for Dimly-bottled Splotnik, a pork-rind liquor with its origins in a tiny Old World Balkan country called Pianvia . . ." Kip said, ". . . well, I don't know too much about that stuff, exactly. But Gram always said it was the 'source of inspiration for an artistic generation.' I think that means hippies liked it."

"Hippies and *my* grandma," Daisy said. "Who,

come to think of it, was probably a hippie. Huh."

"Is that where you get *your* inspiration?" He gestured at Daisy's hat and the rest of her outfit.

Daisy didn't seem the least bit offended. She just grinned and nodded. "Yeah," she said. "My grandma's kinda nuts, y'know? Always quoting old Pianvian proverbs to me. But she's cool too. We get along."

"She still in Dimly?"

Daisy nodded, a faraway look in her eyes. "Yeah . . ."

"So how come you're not?"

"Oh. Uh." She frowned. "I'm . . . I'm still not really sure." Her lip trembled a bit.

"Hey," Kip said. "Sorry. You don't have to tell me. I was just curious."

"I know." She took a deep breath and sighed. "Actually, curious is nice. You're the first kid I've met here who's bothered to actually take an interest."

"Yeah, well, you're the first kid who's seen me parkour and not pointed and laughed."

"I was only going to do that if you were dead." She grinned. "I'm not heartless."

Kip laughed. Daisy was cool. "So . . . why the new digs?" he asked. "On the run from the Mob?"

"Yeah . . . I dunno."

"Okay. Cool. You don't want to talk abo—"

"No, Kip." She looked at him. "I actually *don't*

know. See, a little over a year ago I was living in Dimly, going to school, hanging out with my best friend, Jess — and generally just being Daisy Kildare of Dimly the Dull."

"So . . . ?"

"So," Daisy continued, "one night I woke up and thought the auto shop up the street must have caught fire. All I could smell was burnt rubber."

"Gag."

"Seriously. It woke me up from a sound sleep." She frowned, her eyebrows knitting together. "I remember I'd been having this really weird dream about somebody in a panda suit standing over my bed, whispering and laughing. And then suddenly my mom burst into my room, waving a lightsaber and yelling like a maniac, and the panda dove out the window headfirst."

"Weird dream!" Kip said. "I only ever get bears on bicycles—"

"No." Daisy shook her head. "*That* part was real. My mom likes sci-fi conventions. She won a working lightsaber one year in a costume contest."

"Ah. Okay then. Carry on."

"Well, next thing I know," Daisy continued, "I'm on a plane with my mom who acts like nothing's wrong. 'It's just time to move on,' she says. 'Change of scenery.'" Daisy shrugged. "Well, what's a Daisy gonna do? She's my mom. So, I decided okay, I'll come along for the ride and see what happens."

"Your uh . . . dad?"

Daisy shrugged again. "Not in the picture." She said it in a way that let Kip know to let that subject drop.

"It's all a little weird, Kildare."

She sighed. "I was used to weird. Come to think of it, all of that went down after the *usual* weirdness."

"Do I even want to ask?" Kip gave her a sideways look.

Daisy hesitated. Kip waited. And when she slipped off her knapsack, sitting beside it on a patch of grass under the tree, he sank down cross-legged to listen.

"The Burnt Rubber Panda Dream Incident," she began, "happened the day after we got home from this annual crazy trip I used to have to take to Montreal."

Kip nodded. "I've heard Montreal's pretty crazy—"

"No, no. Montreal's fine." She waved a hand dismissively. "Great smoked-meat sandwiches. No, I mean, the trip *itself* was the crazy part."

He'd only just met her, true. And it was far-out unbelievable, sure. But something about the way Daisy told it . . . well, Kip believed every word. He settled himself down with his back to the tree and gestured for her to continue.

CHAPTER 4

A TALE OF ONE WEIRDO

(D)aisy had never been able to talk about the annual treks from Dimly to Montreal with anyone other than Jess, who'd had to suffer through them too.

The whole thing was just too bizarre. Year after year, Daisy and her mom would go to Quebec, where a weirdo research specialist named Dr. Edgar Fassbinder from some weirdo government-funded think tank called the "Institut de l'ennui / Boredom Institute" would perform a series of weirdo poky-proddy tests.

Daisy and her mom would return home, where Daisy and Jess would exchange notes . . . and then pretend the visits had never happened as far as anyone else was concerned. Add to that Daisy's mom's *extreme* reluctance to talk about anything to do with Fassbinder or the Boredom Institute — or pandas — and Daisy just never brought it up. With anyone. Ever.

But for some reason Daisy felt like she could confide in Kip. Maybe it was that they both had nutso grandmas. Or that he actually knew where — *what* — Dimly was. Or maybe it was that he was a little weird too, but seemed genuinely nice. Whatever it was, Daisy didn't get the impression Kip would turn around and snicker about her with his friends once she was gone.

"The place reeks of Gorgonzola and garlic," Daisy said, trying to describe the weirdness that was the Boredom Institute, that dingy office hidden away in the sub-basement of a Montreal hospital. Daisy's mom had taken her there for "gifted testing" every year since she could remember — with no tangible "gifts" ever having presented themselves. A waste of time, Daisy had always thought. But Jess had to go through it too. And Gary. And . . . probably Archie?

"And they have a serious pest-control problem," she continued. "All you can hear when you're in the examination rooms is scurrying and squeaking. And *nothing* ever happens! At least, nothing *usually* happens."

"Usually?" Kip asked, leaning forward.

"Well . . . last time we were there," she said, trying hard to remember the details, "I had to fill out yet another weirdo questionnaire, only somebody had walked off with all the pens. I'm all hooked up to the machines and nobody's around, so I go into my knapsack to get my own. All I've got is this box of pencils from my mom's work . . ."

"And?"

"And, for the first time ever, *something* happens."

Kip leaned farther forward. "What?"

"I get a shock. From the pencil."

"The . . . pencil." Kip leaned back a little. "Okaaay . . ."

"Right?" Daisy shrugged. "It's *so* no big deal but all of a sudden, the machine I'm hooked up to goes bonkers! Beeping and pinging and the needle zigzagging all over the graph paper like there's an earthquake or something."

"Weeeird . . ."

"*Right?* So I drop the pencil, and the machine goes instantly quiet. But the big mirror on the wall ripples — like someone's leaning on the other side — and the scurrying and squeaking in the walls gets *really* loud."

Now it was Daisy's turn to lean forward. After all those months of not having anyone — not even Jess — to tell her tale to, the details came pouring out of her like a ghost story told around a campfire, weird and spooky-cool. "And then I can hear Fassbinder and my mom talking in the waiting room. Then they're yelling. Then the door opens, Mom busts in all crazy eyes, grabs me, tears off all the wire-stickies — which, *ouch!* — hauls me out of the institute, throws me into the car, and drives like a maniac back to Dimly. Like, non-stop."

"Non-stop? That's a heck of a drive!"

"I know!" Daisy nodded emphatically. "The only time she stops is at a Timmy's for a whole tray of double doubles. And then, get *this*, when we're walking back to the car, I see this . . . thing. In the sky."

"Thing?"

"I'd call it a blimp," Daisy said, instinctively checking the empty sky overhead, "but that'd be an insult to the average blimp. This thing looks more like a football that's been kicked around by a water buffalo wearing golf spikes. It's patched in so many places it's more patch than blimp. And it's droopy and lopsided and farting black smoke all over the sky—"

"I get it," Kip grinned. "A derelict dirigible."

"Of detestable demeanour, yeah." Daisy snorted and grinned back. "Anyway, Mom spots it too, body-checks me down behind a camper van, and makes me hide there until it putt-farts away over the horizon. Next thing I know, I'm back in Dimly. Briefly."

"Then it's burnt-rubber, panda-suit dreams," Kip concluded, "and suddenly you're the new kid in a new school on the other side of the country."

"Yup." Daisy nodded. "With an unlisted phone number."

Kip looked at her sideways. "Do you . . . Do you think, maybe, this has something to do with your dad?" he asked tentatively.

"I think it's got more to do with me." She shrugged, at a loss to explain. "I just don't know what."

"Well, at least you don't have to deal with that anymore."

"Yeah. If I never hear anything more about Doc Fassbinder or the Boredom Institute or gifted testing ever again, it'll be too soon."

Kip glanced at the sky then too. The sun had reappeared, but who could guess for how long. "I gotta go," he said, reluctantly.

Daisy nodded. "Me too."

"Hey," Kip said, before they parted ways on Comox Street, "you picked a camp for the long weekend yet?"

"Nah. This morning I was pretty sure I had my destiny all figured out, but now . . . I dunno." She glanced at Kip sideways, at his scuffed jeans and the scrapes on his elbows from his failed parkouring. "I don't have a calling, I guess."

Kip grinned at her. "How can you have a calling when you've got an unlisted number?"

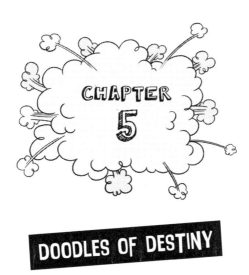

CHAPTER 5

DOODLES OF DESTINY

When Daisy got home from school, her mom greeted her from the kitchen with a cheery "Hi, hon!" and the smell of baking cookies. Snickerdoodles. Daisy's absolute fave. And something that, in Daisy's experience, was generally reserved for celebratory occasions. Or as an antidote to "Pianvian Meat Loaf Nights," when Daisy's grandmother — lovable, eccentric Granny Florie (one-and-a-half cats shy of official Crazy Cat Lady status) — would visit. Granny Florie's special *gag* meat loaf recipe was always served with a drizzled sauce made from a reduction of *double gag* Splotnik. The only thing that ever rid the kitchen of the lingering Splotniky stench was the aroma of baking cookies.

So. Snickerdoodles. On a non-meat-loaf occasion. Something was up. And it wasn't Daisy's birthday, because she and her mom had already celebrated that early, a couple of days ago, with a shopping-spree trip to the Granville Island market, where Daisy had scored a fringed vest that complemented her floppy hippie hat, which had come from Granny Florie herself. And there'd been the birthday cupcake tucked in with her lunch that morning. So yeah. Birthday shenanigans had already been ticked off the agenda.

The cookies? This had to be something else entirely. Side-eyeing the kitchen doorway, Daisy plucked off her hat and hung it on the hallstand.

"I. Am. SO. Proud. Of. You!" Daisy's mom exclaimed in little staccato bursts as she skipped — seriously, *skipped* — in from the kitchen to kiss Daisy on the top of her head for emphasis. "Oh, honey, what on earth happened to your hair?" Mom blinked and tilted her head. "Well. Never mind! I baked cookies to celebrate. Come, eat!"

Then she was gone, skipping — seriously, *skipping* — back into the kitchen. Proud of what? Celebrate what? Daisy kicked off her shoes and shrugged out of her knapsack — and did a double take when she caught a glimpse of her reflection in the hall mirror. And then a *triple* take! What *had* happened to her hair?! She realized she hadn't looked in a mirror since sometime before lunch, but whoa! Her normally mildly wavy locks resembled a ball of yarn that had been left unattended in a basket of kittens. Bits and pieces corkscrewed wildly out from her scalp in all directions. Daisy frowned and patted uselessly at the tangled strands, muttering, "Stupid Vancouver humidity . . . " As she made her way to the kitchen to discover the source of the celebratory cookie goodness, she marvelled at how Kip had somehow managed to avoid making fun of her loopy locks.

The source was, apparently, her acceptance into Art Camp — on *full* scholarship — for the May Long Weekend Campstravaganza.

"Wha—?" was her initial response when her mom told her the good news.

"I didn't even know you'd applied!" Mom said.

"Neither did I," Daisy murmured under her breath.

"I didn't even know you could draw!"

"Neither did *I.*"

Daisy reached for a snickerdoodle, lost in confusion. But as she chewed the warm, gooey goodness, she recalled her strange encounter at school that morning with Archie and the art teacher. Both of whom — Daisy had concluded — had been mocking her for her lack of artistic ability. *Not* signing her up for camp! She mumbled a mouthful of answers to her mom's giddy questions as she scooted back into the hall to retrieve the card she'd doodled on for Jess from her knapsack. But then she remembered she'd already mailed it on the way home.

All that was left in the pocket of her knapsack was her pencil and a travel pack of tissues — holdovers from when she used to hang out with Jess, whose prodigious allergies were the stuff of Dimly legend. For a second, as her fingers brushed the pencil, Daisy imagined she felt a *tingle* along her knuckles. Her frown deepened as she stared accusingly at the back of her hand. Her other hand slowly drifted up to snarl in the tangles of her hair . . .

She shook her head sharply and then flapped her hands like she was shaking water droplets from her fingers.

No. That's ridiculous, she thought.

But then she thought, *Yeah? Well so is me going to Art Camp.* But ridiculous or not, that was exactly what was going to happen. In less than a week. Gulp.

CHAPTER 6

HAPPY(ISH) CAMPERS

Kip made it home that day just in time to feed Percy without there being any dire repercussions. Percy, due to the unfortunate circumstances of his origins, was not to be held responsible for the kind of property damage he could inflict when hungry.

"There you go, buddy," Kip said, pouring a generous measure of kibble into a bowl by the back door.

Percy was a three-legged, one-eyed rescue marmot that Kip's mom had brought home from Vancouver Animal Rescue Services three years earlier, when she'd gone to do a day of doggy art therapy with some of the more anxiety-prone pups in residence. Mrs. Winklehorn had watched a documentary on animal artists — apes, elephants and dolphins whose trainers had taught them to paint — and she'd convinced the VARS folks that an afternoon running around on sheets of brown paper with their paws dipped in non-toxic tempera paint would relax some of the jitterier pups — with the added bonus of being able to sell the paintings to help support the service.

It had gone over like gangbusters and was now a regular gig for Kip's mom, in addition to her duties as the school art teacher and the director of the May Long Weekend Art Camp. But on that first visit to the rescue facility, she'd been in the lobby when a park ranger brought in Percy. A young marmot, he'd somehow run afoul of some off-season ski-lift equipment undergoing maintenance and, in the process, gotten himself chewed up pretty badly.

Huddled in a cat carrier, Percy's (one-eyed) mournful gaze had met Kip's mom's and, well, that was that. She'd donated her entire honorarium for the doggy art therapy session to his medical bills and, once he was fully (well, as fully as possible) recovered, brought him home as a pet for Kip. A three-legged, one-eyed, half-an-eared, scruffy-as-all-get-out pet.

Percy never seemed to begrudge his lot in life. He was, in fact, the happiest — ugliest — little critter Kip had ever known. Smart too. And he was a good pal. Which was what Kip needed after checking the messages on the home phone, only to discover that he'd been rejected from Parkour Camp. Again. This time without even having to fail the entrance test first.

"Oh, Kip, sweetie," his mom said when she got home and found him sharing a pint of rocky road ice cream with Percy. "I'm sorry. Well, look on the bright side. You can come to Art Camp again this year! You're so talented, dear, and always such a big help to me . . ." She clasped her hands. "And there's only one spot left — I filled the second-last one today with a very promising candidate!"

"You did?"

"Out of the blue!" she said. Her brow creased faintly and she tapped her pale purple nails on the counter. "Some girl named . . . Dahlia, I think. Or Daylily. It's all a little hazy. Delphinium . . . ?"

Kip sat up and blinked. "Daisy?"

"That's it!"

Huh, Kip thought. *Interesting . . . Promising candidate?* And yet, earlier today she'd known nothing about her hometown's contribution to the art world.

Kip scooped up another spoonful of ice cream and fed it to a gleefully chirping Percy. *There is way more to Daisy Kildare than meets the eye,* he thought, recalling the crazy story she'd told him that afternoon. *Maybe,* Kip thought, *Art Camp won't be as deadly dullsville as usual.*

Little did Kip, or Kip's mom — or, for that matter, Percy — know just how right he was.

Kip didn't see Daisy at school in the days leading up to the Campstravaganza weekend — even though he kept an eye out for her floppy hat and her, uh . . . *unique* hairstyle. But she was one of the first kids he saw getting off the bus when it pulled up to the camp gate on the Friday morning. Pendrell Public, in conjunction with the camp programs, had made it a tradition to extend the long weekend, so it stretched from Friday morning to Monday evening. And every camp jammed their schedules with activity after activity so that when students returned to class on

Tuesday they were all zombified, as well as sporting brand new math skill sets and/or bruises and/or paint stains and/or manuscript drafts to show for their camp efforts.

It clearly wasn't something Daisy had experienced in Dimly, Kip figured, as she stepped off the bus with an expression of extreme uncertainty and stood there in the dusty road. Poor kid looked completely lost, white-knuckle clutching what looked to be a brand new sketch pad to her chest as the rest of the campers streamed around her, chattering and laughing.

"Daisy!" Kip waved. "Yo, Kildare!"

She blinked at the sound of her name and looked around. A smile of relief brightened up her face as she spotted Kip and trotted toward him.

"Hey!" she said. "What are you doing here? I thought you were off to Ninja Camp or whatever."

"Yeah. Well . . ." He shrugged.

"Oh." Her expression twisted into understanding and sympathy. "That's a bummer."

Kip shrugged again. "I'm planning on a growth spurt before next year's entrance tryout," he said. "If I can grow my legs, like, six inches longer, I'll be a shoo-in. In the meantime, this is my sixth year here at Art Camp, so I can at least show you the ropes."

"Sixth?" She blinked at him. "You didn't tell me you were an artist!"

"Meh. It's just a genetic quirk," he said. "I get it from my mom. And my gram, I suppose . . ."

Daisy's gaze narrowed and she looked at him sideways. "You any good?"

It was a question Kip hated answering. Because the truth was that he was good. *Really* good. Drawing and painting came as easily to him as breathing. The only problem was, it bored him to tears. At the same time, he didn't want to sound like he was bragging either.

So he tap danced around the question as he gave Daisy the five-cent tour of camp — from bunkhouses to classroom cabins, from the stretch of beach dotted with firepits and picnic tables to the sparkling, mountain-surrounded lake and thick pine forests beyond. Sessions would start that afternoon. Daisy's first class was Basic Sketch Technique 101, taught by none other than Mrs. Winklehorn. Kip's mom.

"Where are *you* going?" she asked when he told her he'd see her later.

"I'm leading a tutorial on chiaroscuro for the third year advanced oil painting class," he said.

"A tutorial on wha . . . ?"

"The old Italian masters developed it — it's a technique for manipulating light and shadow in a painting to render three-dimensional objects realistically."

Daisy was staring at him.

Kip rolled his eyes, his face reddening with art-nerd embarrassment.

"Right," she snorted. "And *you* think your calling is jumping around on fire escapes. Whereas *I* don't even know what I'm doing here! And I sure as heck don't know what chi-chi-whatever-the-heck is or how to go about achieving it. And I doubt I ever will!"

"You'll be fine." He punched her on the shoulder. "Mom'll start you out on something simple. Probably a still-life sketch of a bowl of fruit. Just . . . draw what you see."

Daisy snorted again. "Right."

She waved at Kip as he turned and loped away, jumping up to kick off a small boulder in the rock garden . . . and falling flat on his face.

❋ ❋ ❋

Daisy watched Kip pick himself up, dust himself off, and trot down the path to disappear between two cabins. And it wasn't long after when Daisy realized that she possessed about the same level of talent as an artist that Kip displayed as a parkour ninja. Zero. *Hoo boy.* It was going to make for a loooong long weekend.

"Sign your finished sketches and leave them on the front table," Mrs. Winklehorn instructed her class of eager young artists. "I'll collect them later. Now . . . *explore* your style! Be bold! Be super! Be sketchy!"

Daisy's stomach growled. It had been a couple of hours since she'd eaten and she could use a snack. Maybe when no one was looking she could sneak a banana from one of the still-life arrangements.

But in the meantime, there was art to be . . . arted. For the next thirty minutes, silence descended on the room, broken only by the sounds of pencil points scratching on paper. Daisy kept stealing glances at the other kids' pads as varying styles of fruit bowls appeared as if by magic. One by one, the other kids finished their drawings and turned them in, heading out into the sunshine and leaving Daisy alone in the cabin — with a blank sketch pad and a sinking feeling in her stomach to replace the hunger growlies.

I shouldn't be here, she thought. There'd been a mistake. A big one.

"C'mon, Kildare," she admonished herself. "Destiny, remember? Something got you into Art Camp, now you just have to prove you belong."

She stared so hard at the fruit bowl her forehead twisted into a knot between her eyebrows. The tip of her tongue stuck out of the corner of her mouth. Beads of sweat formed on the back of her neck. Her knuckles popped as she gripped the pencil. And . . . she was off! Scribbling like a maniac. She bypassed sketching the bowl and went straight for the fruit perched on the top of the arrangement. A pineapple.

As the final pencil stroke completed the outline of her subject, Daisy felt a powerful electric jolt from her fingertips all the way up into the centre of her skull — just like when she'd drawn her doodle for Jess, only it was *way* more powerful this time.

The *ZzAApp!* felt like actually getting hit by lightning, and it was followed by a *POW!!* that seemed as if all of her molecules had exploded outward and then collapsed inward, mashing together in unfamiliar ways. Just like before, Daisy opened her eyes, unravelled her brow-knitting, and peered at her masterpiece.

Or she would have.

If she still had eyes.

Or brows.

Or a masterpiece.

CHAPTER 7

FRUIT LOOPY

"Hey, Daisy," Kip called out in greeting as he did a kick-jump off the door frame of Art Cabin A (bashing his elbow in the process but ignoring the jolt of pain from his funny bone). "How'd it go? You make a masterpiece?"

There was no answer. Kip glanced around the cabin. Empty. Even though he was sure he'd seen Daisy — her hair was really impossible to miss — as he'd passed by the window. She'd been sitting at the big table only a few seconds earlier. And there was only one door. And only one room.

"Daisy?" he called out softly. "Hey . . . Kildare . . ."

He thought he heard a faint, far-off sounding *meep* noise. And a sound like paper crinkling. But the room was still definitely empty. Well, except for the knapsack and sketch pad and pencil case in front of the empty seat that had been pulled out from the table. And the bowls of fruit the class had been using as the subjects for their still-life sketch exercise.

And the really hideously deformed pineapple that had obviously rolled off one of the carefully arranged displays and now sat between a fruit bowl and the abandoned sketch pad.

"Huh," Kip muttered, as he went to pick the thing up and return it to the bowl. "That is one ugly pizza fixin' . . ."

To be fair, it was. Unlike the average tropical delight — like, say, the perfectly proportioned pineapple *already* perched atop the still-life bowl — *this* pineapple was squat and dented and all scribbly-wobbly around the edges. The hash-mark lines that should have criss-crossed its outer skin weren't uniform in the slightest. And the crown that on the average pineapple would have been an orderly green spray of spiky-edged leaves looked an awful lot like a seasick hedgehog that had gone through a spin cycle in the wash on *this* particular fruit.

Kip uttered a "yeesh" before hefting the thing. He was about to return it to the bowl when he noticed the sketch on the pad beside the malformed fruit.

Glancing back and forth, he realized that the sketch didn't so much resemble the fruit . . . as the *fruit* resembled the *sketch*.

And, to put it kindly, the sketch was awful. It was as if someone had taped a pencil to an out-of-water goldfish and let the thing flop around on the paper for a while to see if it could draw. It couldn't. And neither could the person who'd actually done the sketch. Kip flipped the sketch pad closed and read the name written carefully on the front cover in neat block letters: *Daisy Kildare.*

"Meep."

Oh — another thing about regular pineapples versus the one Kip held in his hand? They didn't go "meep."

"Did you just *meep*?" Kip asked the pineapple, and immediately felt fairly silly for doing so. And yet . . . And yet, he could have sworn that the thing was *looking* at him. Not that it had eyes. It was more a sensation that, if it *had* had eyes, they would have been gazing at him. Mournfully. Maybe even a bit desperately. It reminded him of something. And its crown of fronds sproinging out in all directions *definitely* reminded him of something. Of someone. Of . . .

"Daisy?"

"Meep!"

"Oh, gosh!" Startled, Kip fumbled the homely fruit and almost dropped it. "Sorry! Sorry!"

Holy moly, he thought to himself. *Daisy? No. That's not possible.* And it wasn't. But Kip knew deep down that — possible or not — Daisy had somehow managed to turn herself into a tropical fruit. And Kip wasn't about to just leave her there to ripen.

From a philosophical standpoint, Daisy supposed it was an interesting thought experiment to spend some time experiencing life as a tropical fruit. To travel around tucked away in her own knapsack, where Kip had shoved her along with her art supplies. Able to see, but without eyes. Able to hear, but without ears. And smelling like some kind of deliciously scented bath bomb from that store in the mall.

From a *practical* standpoint, however, Daisy didn't think it was interesting at all. More like terrifying. The knapsack was dark and uncomfortable. And her nose itched. At least, the place where her nose used to be . . .

But when Kip finally dumped her out onto the counter in the cabin he shared with his mom, Daisy breathed a sigh of relief. At least she would have but, y'know, no nostrils. Still, for a moment the screeching sense of panic that had gripped her since the whole *ZzAApp! POW!!* thing faded, and she took stock of what was actually happening. She knew she'd been transformed somehow. And even though she was aware that, in her present state, she didn't have eyes or ears or a nose or a mouth, she could somehow still see and hear and smell and, well, "meep." But everything was distorted. Sounds were all echoey, and when Kip leaned over to peer at her, it was like she was looking back at him through a fish-eye lens. His nose looked huge and his ears seemed very far away.

And then he poked her in the "eye" with a giant finger.

"Meep!"

"Sorry!"

"Kip!"

Daisy watched Kip jump a foot in the air at the sound of his mom's voice. He spun around, grabbed the knapsack, and flopped it over to cover Pineapple-Daisy.

"Kip?" Mrs. Winklehorn called again. "Are you in there? I need help bringing in some canvases and supplies from the van."

"Sure, Mom," Kip called back. "Be right there." He spun back to the pineapple. "*Don't* go anywhere, okay? I mean . . . Clearly you're not going anywhere. I know that. And I'm talking to a fruit."

His voice faded into the distance as he went to go help his mom, leaving Daisy alone on the counter, under a knapsack, thinking to herself that maybe Art Camp wasn't going to be anywhere near as boring as she'd thought. And wishing like heck it was.

CHAPTER 8

A DICEY SITUATION

"MOM! STOP!" Kip lunged across the kitchen counter (in a move that, ironically, was one of the ones he'd failed to execute on each of his Parkour Camp tryouts) and yoinked the pineapple out from under the descending blade of a cleaver. Skidding to a halt, Kip held the pineapple close, shielding it from Mrs. Winklehorn's unwitting attempt at culinary carnage. After unloading the art supplies from the van, he'd made it back into the cabin barely in the nick of time to stop his mom from perpetrating pineapple-cide!

"Kip Quentin Winklehorn!" she exclaimed. "I almost chopped your arm off! What on earth were you doing? Is this more of your parkette nonsense?"

"No!" Kip protested, patting Pineapple-Daisy reassuringly. "And it's park*our.* But . . . no. No, Mother, I—" Kip rummaged frantically through a mental list of excuses. Then, drawing himself up to his full height, he faced her and spoke in what he hoped was a tone of grave sincerity "—I have embraced my Art Camp destiny."

"You . . . ? Wait." Mrs. Winklehorn blinked. "What?"

"Art Camp." He blew his bangs out of his eyes and gazed at her with what he hoped was a sufficiently artsy gaze. "It's my jam. My thing. I'm arting. Okay?"

She frowned, processing this new information, a fragile — *wary* — gleam of hope growing behind her eyes. "I mean — you're so talented, hon, but I thought you just did this to help me out every year."

"*Pff*." Kip waved off the suggestion. "I'm an *artiste*, Mother. I'm allowed, nay *expected*, to be temperamental. From, er, time to time."

"Oh. Oh! Well, okay — from time to time, I guess." She raised an eyebrow. "But what's with the pineapple pilfering?"

"Uh . . . secret project. I'm in the conceptualizing stages."

"Oh, sweetie!" Mrs. Winklehorn *tsked*, reaching for the thing. "I can get you a much nicer-looking pineapple than that. *That* one's only good for dicing into the salad—"

"No!" Kip recoiled, backing up until his shoulders were jammed against the pantry doors.

"Okaaay . . ." She lifted the cleaver in a gesture of surrender and turned her attention to a pomegranate, hacking it in half with one fell stroke of the blade. Kip swore he felt Daisy flinch.

"Who knew?" His mom continued chopping fruit into a big glass bowl, muttering to herself. "My son, the avant-garde master. Well, at least he's less likely to get himself into life-threatening danger this way."

Little did Mrs. Winklehorn know. Little did Kip know. Little did Daisy . . . Aw, you get the picture. Nobody knew anything about what was going to happen at this point. Well, *almost* nobody . . .

CHAPTER 9

OF MICE AND MINIONS

"I am *not* a nobody," Dr. Gavin Bafflegab muttered to himself as he clomped down the rough-hewn stone stairs leading to his hidden underground lair (tripping only on the last step, an improvement on his usual routine, which involved several missteps and a banged shin or stubbed toe). "Nobody calls me a nobody! Especially not those buffoons at the university! *They're* the nobodies."

"Well," the lab-coated rat scampering down the stairs beside him said in an off-key squeak, "seeing as how they're the ones calling you a nobody and you just called them nobodies and said that nobody calls you a nobody . . . wouldn't that mean that they did? And you are?"

Bafflegab screeched to a halt and glared down at his nefarious hench-varmint. "Gerald," he said through gritted teeth, "leave the thinking to those of us with actual thought processes. Please."

"Right, Doc." Gerald rolled his beady little eyes and stuffed the tiny pad holding the draft notes for his quantum theory research paper back into the side pocket of his tiny lab coat. "No processing here. Not a bit of it."

He admirably resisted the urge to sink his long yellow teeth into Bafflegab's ankle and instead turned his frustration inward, mentally rolling it up into a tiny ball of slow-burning rage and adding it to all the other tiny, fiery rage balls he'd accumulated. It was a visualization technique Gerald had taught himself by watching YouTube videos. One day, when he'd collected enough tiny rage balls in his mental tiny-rage-ball basket, he would unleash them and wreak his not-so-tiny revenge.

Revenge for what? you might ask. And on whom? you might ponder. Well, the "what" was having been transformed, against his will, into a mutant super genius with global domination aspirations and no opposable thumbs to speak of. It made holding a pencil (even a tiny golf pencil) really hard, and thus Gerald's genius — as scrawled on his tiny notepads — remained unintelligible to anyone but himself.

The "whom" was a doctor, Dr. Edgar Fassbinder of the Boredom Institute, and his precious little gang of mouse lab assistants. Thought they were all so darn smart, they did. Mousy superiority complexes, the lot of them. Especially that Algernon creep with his fancy cheese trays and his groan-worthy puns. Claude had been the only one out of the whole lot of them with whom Gerald felt any kind of kinship. Claude was smart enough to be dissatisfied. Conniving. Claude got it. He was looking for his own way out of a life of boredom.

When Doc Fassbinder had first started experimenting with the highly unstable, wildly volatile element reidium, his laboratory had also housed a bank of cages filled with lab animals (a bunch of run-of-the-mill white mice and a single, solitary, utterly ordinary rat, to be specific). Over time, the cages had become increasingly contaminated with trace amounts of the reidium. The cumulative effects on the lab inhabitants was . . . unexpected. Extraordinary. Groundbreaking. Pretty nifty. It accelerated the intelligence capabilities of the rodenty little fellows and boosted their sentience quotients into the stratosphere.

In short, it made them smart. Capable. Strong. Able to communicate, and dress themselves stylishly — not to mention perform all manner of feats of derring-do. It also gave them ambitions, aspirations . . . personality disorders. Well, in Gerald's case, at least. It turned him into a ratty little megalomaniac. Or, as he liked to describe himself to anyone who cared to listen, Eeeeevil. Yes, capital E followed by four lowercase e's.

The mice? As far as Gerald was concerned, it just made them annoying little do-gooders. Especially Algernon. Yeesh. But — and this was the real kicker — Doc Fassbinder had given them all promotions. Made them his assistants. Just because lab mice were somehow more acceptable than lab rats. The discrimination was so blatant.

But Gerald had used the situation to his advantage as best he could. He'd hidden his superior abilities, played the ordinary rat, chewed his carrots slowly, and bided his time. Until one day opportunity presented itself and — in a whirlwind whiff of burnt-rubber stench and maniacal cackling — he'd found his ally: The Boss.

And The Boss had recognized Gerald's talents for what they were. Useful. The Boss had manifested seemingly out of nowhere one dark night, communicating to Gerald through an old transistor radio the clever little rat had been tinkering with, attempting to modify it into a gamma-beta wave receptor and . . . Never mind. It's complicated. All you need to know is that the thing started hissing and crackling one night while all the other lab rodents were busy snoozing. Slackers.

"*FiiiizzZzzzZZz . . . Ger—ld.*" The speaker sizzled in the darkness. "*Come in, G—rald . . . zzZZiiZZzz.*"

Gerald scrambled for the tuning dial and volume knob. "Who — what — uh, yes! Gerald here. Over. Uh, I mean, roger. I mean . . . who is this?!"

The voice came in a little clearer as he fiddled with the frequency tuner. Enough for Gerald to discern a somewhat smoky quality to it. Like a tire fire. But he couldn't tell if it came from a man or a woman.

"*You may call me The Boss,*" it said. "*I have a job for a rodent of your particular ssskill ssset,*" the disembodied voice hissed in a sibilant whisper.

Gerald blinked at the speaker, bemused.

"Unlesssss, of courssssse, you're content with your current lot in life—"

"No!" he squeaked, then glanced around to make sure he hadn't woken any of his lab mates. "No! I'm listening . . ."

The voice — and it sounded Eeeeevil enough that Gerald was convinced of its nefarious purposes — informed him that his mission would mean freedom from Fassbinder's lab.

"But . . . where would I go?" Gerald asked.

"Rural British Columbia," the voice answered. *"There, you will assist Dr. Gavin Bafflegab — one of my multitude of villainous henchmen — in his research. Dr. Bafflegab is . . . shall we say, in rather desperate need of a clever minion."*

If Gerald had eyebrows, he would have raised one rather sharply.

"Well? What do you say?"

Gerald scratched his furry little chin, thinking. It didn't take him long to decide. "I'll do it."

So that was that. Later that night, he awoke to discover a small folded piece of paper next to his water with directions and a schedule for a train he could sneak on to that would get him cross-country.

A little over a week later, he was in the British

Columbian interior, deep below ground, hench-rat and minion to Dr. Gavin Bafflegab. "Minion" was an entry-level position in the world of Eeeeevil villaindom — and The Boss had been a little vague on the details — but under the circumstances, Gerald didn't mind so much.

He was away from the mice. He had his own posh digs, all the premium rat kibble he could possibly want (A pox on fancy cheeses! Bleh!) and ample time to work on his own nefarious quantum research, which was mostly designs for transdimensional mousetraps.

Of course, he'd been curious upon arrival as to what, exactly, Bafflegab did hidden away in his sprawling subterranean complex. But the answer had surprised even him.

"My work here is of vital importance," Bafflegab had informed the rat in a plummy English accent that Gerald suspected might be fake.

"Yes," Gerald had nodded, "so you said. But you haven't, not exactly, said what that work is. If I'm to be of nefarious assistance, certain intel might come in handy. For instance, what the heck is this place?"

"This? This, my dear wee fellow, is . . . the Cryptolair. And I, Dr. Gavin Bafflegab, Esquire, am its lord and master — and cryptozoologist extraordinaire!"

Gerald had to fake a sneezing fit in order not to

laugh outright in Bafflegab's face. Cryptozoology? Of all the quack pseudo-sciences for Gerald to get himself hooked up with! This? This was pure charlatanism! Hoaxes and chicanery! This Bafflegab chap was nothing but a flim-flam man! A bamboozler! A fraud. (Gerald, upon gaining hyperintelligence, had made good use of the out-of-date thesaurus pages Fassbinder had used to line the lab cages.)

"The more narrow-minded members of the scientific community call it a 'pseudo-science,'" Bafflegab sneered as he plucked a tissue from a box on a chrome shelf and handed it to his new lab assistant. "The fools."

"Fatheads!" Gerald agreed, stifling a snicker in the tissue. Really, he was inclined to agree with them. Because what cryptozoology was . . . was ridiculous! Attempting to prove the existence of creatures of folklore and legend. "*Pff!*"

He glanced at the neatly typed labels a row of binders shelved on one wall. *Bigfoot/Sasquatch/Yeti/ Skunk Ape/Etc.* was on the fattest binder; *Loch Ness Monster* was on one almost as fat. Then there was a set of smaller, colour-coordinated binders labelled *Ogopogo, Winnipogo, Manipogo, Igopogo.* They went on and on: *Chupacabra, Mermaids/Mermen/Merfolk, Dragons/Sky Serpents, Ozark Howler, Gremlins/*

Goblins/Imps. The last binder in the row was labelled *Pianvian Wolpertinger — Extremely Elusive! — Classified!* And there were little stars drawn around the word "Classified."

What on earth? Gerald had wondered. He listened with half an ear as Bafflegab gave him the nickel tour. The hideout was located in the Okanagan Valley in B.C. because, for one thing, that's where Ogopogo was said to hang its sea-serpenty hat. But also because Dr. Bafflegab had applied for, and received, funding from an obscure local government science grant sometime in the 1970s — back when that kind of science was a Thing — that the government had probably never gotten around to deactivating.

The more time Gerald spent in Bafflegab's employ, the more he figured Bafflegab was the only one who ever applied for the darn thing and that's why he kept getting it. But, what the heck! Over the years, the accumulated sums had paid for a pretty sweet subterranean lair. And the grant office had yet to ask Bafflegab to produce so much as a scale off Ogopogo's mythical hide.

And so Gerald had stayed. He dutifully ran scans of all sorts, set high-tech cryptid traps in the forest, remote-steered underwater surveillance drones through the cold, dark depths of the mountain lakes, relentlessly combed through tabloid newspapers and websites for any leads that might actually pan out, and listened to Bafflegab's endless rants on how he was an underappreciated genius and a giant in his field. Of course, it would have helped if he were an actual giant. Then they could have claimed to have discovered a real cryptid and called it a day.

But no. Three years into his employment in the Cryptolair, Gerald was getting restless. More to the point, The Boss was getting impatient. An impatience that was being communicated in more and more dire terms to Gerald whenever he reported in (behind the good doctor's back) that a cryptid army of creepy creatures was yet to be forthcoming. Something had to happen. And it had to happen soon.

CHAPTER 10

FRUIT PUNCHED!

"PERCY! Leave that pineapple alone! Gah! Bad marmot! BAD! Drop it!" Kip felt bad yelling at Percy, who couldn't have known any better. After all, Kip's mom routinely brought home still-life fruit that had served its artistic purpose as a treat for the rescue marmot. How was Percy to know *this* particular pineapple was off limits? Except the second Kip admonished him, the marmot backed away from the pineapple as if it had been his idea anyway and looked at it sideways.

It wobbled from side to side on the rug, and Percy peered quizzically at it with his one good eye, his scruffy, wonky-eared head tilted on a sharp angle. Kip watched silently as Percy sat back on his chubby haunches and pawed at it — gently — with his single front paw. Then he looked up at Kip and howl-growled a querulous sound.

"Yeah," Kip sighed. "I know, pal. And you have to keep this *strictly* between the two of us. Er . . . the three of us. Right, Daisy?" Daisy *meeped*. And Percy looked back and forth between the two of them like they were both out of their minds. Which would have made *waaaay* more sense than the truth, Kip thought.

"Well . . . I can't leave you here like that," he said to the forlorn fruit. "But I'm not really sure what to do with you either. I can't exactly tell anyone about this." He frowned in frustration, absently flipping the pages of Daisy's sketch pad. "I wonder how long you're going to stay like that."

The still life was on the first page of the pad. Kip had a feeling that it might be the first serious drawing Daisy had ever attempted, other than the birthday card doodle she'd told him about while he was showing her around the camp grounds — the one that landed her in Art Camp in the first place.

He peered at the pineapple drawing, holding it just under his nose. Up close, the chaotic grey pencil marks didn't look like regular pencil marks. They sparkled. Kind of. In the right light, as Kip tilted the page this way and that, he could see there was a faint, flickering sheen to the lines. He fished through the outer pocket of Daisy's knapsack for the pencil she'd been using in sketch class. At a casual glance, it looked like any normal HB pencil. He read the lettering stamped into the green surface.

"*Dimly Bulb Company*," Kip murmured. "*Where Bright Ideas Come to Life.* Huh."

A hazy theory of how to help Daisy started to take shape in Kip's mind. Impossible? Sure.

But all the evidence pointed to the same conclusion. And the fact that, really, Kip was Daisy's only hope of becoming human again.

The fact that he engaged in a full half hour of pacing before testing his theory didn't mean that he was stalling — no, no — he was just . . . pondering. Running alternate scenarios in his mind. Okay, okay, he was stalling. First chance he had, Kip had vamoosed back to Art Cabin A, Daisy tucked under his arm like a football. Half an hour later, Kip had almost worn a groove in the cabin floor with his nervous pacing. He'd knocked over the same chair at the far end of the room twelve times trying to execute a sideways bounce-leap every time his pacing took him to that side of the cabin. But enough was enough. The situation demanded action. He stopped, huffed out a breath, and stalked back to the table. "Daisy?"

"Meep?"

"You can't stay a pineapple forever. You know that, right?" He pulled up a chair and sat down, determined to convince the inanimate fruit (and, more to the point, himself) of the rightness of his plan.

"Well," he continued, "I don't exactly know how to fix this. But I have an idea. Only it's not risk free." He brandished the sketchbook, open to the pineapple page. "*This* turned you into *that*. Right? It's okay — you don't have to answer. But I think you understand me, and I need your permission to try something. It's kind of an experiment."

With his other hand, he brandished a brand new, never-been-used, sharp-edged Pink Pearl eraser.

Most of the other artists Kip knew used newer plastic or kneadable gum erasers, but Kip's mom swore by Pink Pearls, just like his grandma before her. And as a result, so did he.

"I know you're probably thinking, what if I erase *you*, right?"

"Meep!"

"But look at it this way," he said, walking the pineapple through the logic of his hypothesis. "You existed *before* the drawing. Just like the sketchbook page. It seems to me that what the sketch has done is just . . . just put a disguise on you. Made you *sketchy*, if you know what I mean. Soooooo, if I erase the sketch and erase you along with it, I . . . Well, that's not good. I mean, I—"

"Mip," the pineapple interrupted him (he could have sworn it was trying to say his name that time) and then let out a resigned "meeep." Then the malformed fruit tipped over on its side and rolled toward him. Just a little. Kip blinked. And then nodded. He figured that if Daisy was really against his suggestion, she would have rolled the other way — *away* from him.

"Okay. Okay. I think." He was getting an impatient "dude, let's *do* this thing" vibe from Pineapple-Daisy. He took a deep breath. "Okay!"

"Eeesh." He winced, looking at the drawing on the

page. Daisy really hadn't been kidding when she'd said she didn't belong at Art Camp. Funny how neither of them had wound up in the place they thought they should have. Only maybe, Kip thought, if Daisy really did have some kind of gift — some far-out ability to transform into things — maybe she *did* belong there. Or somewhere, at least. Somewhere she could learn to use her powers. Maybe that was what Kip was there for. Maybe there was a reason Parkour Camp had so resoundingly rejected him.

"Whatever," he muttered, as he rolled up his sleeves. "It's gotta be more fun than bruise collecting, right?"

Carefully at first, and then with slightly more frantic swipes of the Pink Pearl eraser, Kip went to work obliterating the image of the mutant fruit, half in a panic that his efforts would actually obliterate the person who'd sketched it.

There was a moment of stillness, then *zZOiNKk! sCRAKk! waAkKOOo!* followed by a flash of greenish-grey light. And Kip looked up from the once-again blank page to find Daisy, scrunched up in what looked like an impossible yoga pose, sitting on the table in front to him. Wide-eyed and grimacing.

"D–Daisy?"

"Mip?" she squeaked. "I mean, Kip?"

She twitched a bit convulsively and unfolded

herself from the knot of knees and elbows she was contorted into. Then she scrambled off the table, hopping around awkwardly for a few seconds as if not quite believing that she was person shaped again. She turned to him, still wide-eyed.

"Kip!" she yelped, and threw herself at him in a frantic, flaily bear hug. "KIP! Thank-you-thank-you-thank-you!" she exclaimed. "I thought I was doomed!"

Kip blushed and untangled himself from the hug. "I'm just really glad it worked," he said.

"You and me both."

He grinned. "Wanna try it again?"

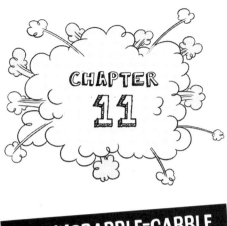

CHAPTER 11

TECHNOBABBLE-GABBLE

For a moment upon entering the Cryptolair's main lab, Gerald wondered if ol' Baffles hadn't *finally* discovered an *actual* cryptid. The image projected on the big screen suspended above the computer console was grainy, the signal relaying it obviously weak or experiencing interference, and the image certainly looked like a monsterish creature of some sort.

But when the transmission cleared briefly, Gerald saw that it looked more like a dinosaur — a cheap, rubbery *Tyrannosaurus rex*. And then it spoke, and he realized that it was The Boss. In a dinosaur suit. The eyeholes looked empty but still somehow managed to convey annoyance. In the background, Gerald thought he saw something that looked like a deflated giant panda draped over a chair. The Boss had an . . . *unusal* fashion sense.

"*I'm not seeing progress, Gavin.*" The voice crackled and hissed, drifting out like oily, gritty smoke through the expensive surround-sound system. Gerald had finally figured out that The Boss was a boss *lady*. But a lady who, he suspected, gargled with Tabasco sauce or took her coffee mixed with battery acid. The grating tones of her voice were painful to listen to. "All I'm seeing is you lounging around in the kind of primo digs I should be occupying, while I'm stuck up here in this third-rate patchwork blimp! You're wasting my money!"

"Now, now, my dear. I'm wasting the *government's* money. And I assure you, it looks far more posh than it is here. This —" Bafflegab waved his hand at the gleaming chrome and leather furnishings, the state-of-the-art electronics, the banks of monitors and the (over-the-top, Gerald *had* warned him) sparkling crystal chandeliers hanging from the rough-hewn stone of the cavern roof "— it's all set dressing. Cardboard and Styrofoam. Green-screen digital effects! Only so I can continue to receive the grant money for our important and truly nefarious work! Were you to visit the Cryptolair yourself, you'd see it's barely more than a mole hole down here and—"

Gerald took that opportune moment to roll the happy hour bar cart into view of the camera. He had a somewhat twisted sense of humour.

"Er, yes. Thank you, Gerald." Bafflegab tried his best to nudge the cart out of the frame with his foot. "Not now. I'll examine the, er, chemical solutions in those, um, beakers later."

"But of course, Doctor. Oh! Why, greetings, Your Bossfulness," Gerald said, as if just that moment noticing the image on the screen. He executed a gentlemanly bow. "Looking good, ma'am. Very stylish. The scales and teeth suit you. Brings out your eyes . . ."

The empty dinosaur eyeholes swung in his direction. "*Ah, Gerald.*" The Boss's voice turned threatening. "*Report! Am I any closer to having an army of sasquatches at my disposal? A navy of sea serpents? A marine corps of mermaids? Hmm? Well? Where, I ask, are my cadres of chupacabras? My phalanxes of flying monkeys?"*

Where, indeed? Gerald wondered. He didn't believe in Bafflegab's cryptozoology nonsense for a hot-potato second. And he was pretty sure that last thing The Boss had mentioned was a monster from *The Wizard of Oz.* But he also didn't want to lose his cushy gig and access to all of the Cryptolair's technology for his own purposes. So he lied.

"Dr. Bafflegab is far too modest," Gerald said, hopping up onto the bar cart and nudging the scientist over with his little elbow. "Allow *me*, then, to expound on the excellence of his progress."

"The what of my what?" Bafflegab interjected.

"We received 'pings' earlier in the week!" Gerald enthused.

"Pings?" The Boss asked warily.

"We did?" Bafflegab frowned.

"Sure!" Gerald nodded emphatically. "Radar, sonar, echolocation, radiowave, microwave, uh . . . all that stuff. Multiple pings. Many different targets. It'll take time to track them all down but we have a . . . a working theory! Yes, that's it! They're all interconnected somehow. A network of cryptids. And if we can tap into that network, it will revolutionize the field. We can track them, hunt them, capture them ... and, in the process, make you not only rich but powerful beyond imagining."

Of course, Gerald was *totally* making all that stuff up. He didn't believe a word of his own words. There were no "pings." Bafflegab had so far come up with zilch. But Gerald's bogus report was delivered with such convincing panache that even ol' Baffles was almost inclined to believe it.

"Yes! Yes. The pings! Of course," he enthused. "I was preparing a full briefing, but Gerald here has cracked right to the nut of the matter. We're on the cusp of a breakthrough." Bafflegab yammered on, peppering in enough technobabble that eventually The Boss grudgingly praised them for their fine work and said she would leave them to it. At least, she threatened, until she could manage to pilot her aging blimp out to the West Coast to see the results for herself.

In the moment, Gerald's genius improvisation had managed to stave off the wrath of The Boss and save Bafflegab's skin. But his performance also set in motion a series of events that even his brilliant rat brain couldn't have begun to imagine. Because what Gerald, perched atop the bar cart, had failed to notice was the long, twisting shadow slithering through the cold, dark lake, past the floor-to-ceiling underwater observation windows of the Cryptolair. And what he couldn't have heard, even if he *had* noticed, was the subsonic wave that travelled through the waters of Lake Okanagan and out into the wide world beyond, carrying a message. And that message was: *Guys . . . I think they're on to us . . .*

"It's a working theory."

"Uh huh."

"*Pff.*" Kip waved away Daisy's negativity.

The two of them had met after parting ways for an hour so that Kip could fire up the kiln for the Advanced Pottery class and Daisy could (reluctantly) attend her Introduction to Origami class, where she had managed to fold a reasonably decent paper crane without, she'd been enormously relieved to discover, turning into one.

"I want credit when you become an internet sensation," Kip continued. "The technical term for what you do — y'know, if there was actually a technical term for it — is . . . get this . . . transmogrification!"

"Huh?"

"You transmogrify." He accompanied the word with a little flourish of jazz hands.

Daisy glared at Kip balefully. "Why do you even know what that is?"

"I follow the Merriam-Webster Dictionary Twitter feed." He shrugged. "It was the word of the day a couple of weeks ago."

Daisy gave Kip a look. "And this particular bit of technobabble *means* . . . ?"

"It means to drastically change or alter in appearance . . ."

Daisy snorted. "Well, I can't really argue with that—"

". . . in a surprising or, um, magical manner."

She blinked. "Okay, still reasonably accurate—"

"Often in a, um, humorous or . . . uh, y'know, *grotesque* fashion."

"Now, that's just rude." Daisy sighed. "Great. I'm grotesque. Which is just a fancy way of saying gross."

"Not *you*, doofus." Kip punched her on the shoulder. "More like it's your, y'know, 'sketchies' that are grotesque. That's what I'm gonna call the things you transmogrify into from now on. 'Sketchies.' Catchy, huh? And to be fair, it was a pretty ugly pineapple. I shoulda taken a phone pic."

"Ugh."

"But — hey! — magical!"

"I don't *believe* in magic, Kip." Daisy huffed in

frustration. "And neither do you! There has to be another explanation for my . . . grotesqueness."

"Your transmogrificative abilities," he corrected. "*I* think it sounds cool."

She glanced at him sideways. "You can call it whatever you want, but we still don't have a clue *why* or *how* this is happening to me!"

Kip opened his mouth to respond, but he shut it again and shook his head. He was trying to stay upbeat, she knew, but he really didn't know.

She took a subtle sniff of her crazy hair. It still smelled faintly of pineapple. One of the really weird things when Daisy had been in her prickly-fruit state was that she'd been *aware* of her surroundings. Even though everything had been glazed with a persistent high-level panic, she'd understood that Kip had been, well, kind of a hero for her in her hour of fruity need.

She owed him. Big time. But she was also getting frustrated sitting across from him at a picnic table, trying to figure out what the heck was *up* with her. Kip muttered a lot. To himself. She had to keep asking him what he was talking about as he frowned and poked and prodded at her sketch pad, her pencil case, a handful of various pencils and the precious Pink Pearl eraser that had returned her to human form.

"You're muttering. Again," Daisy told him, plucking

up the Dimly Bulb pencil and twirling it between her fingers.

Kip shook his head. "Sorry."

But then it was Daisy's turn to mutter. When Kip asked her what she was saying, she realized she was staring intently at the sharpened point of the pencil. She blinked and tore her gaze away to focus on Kip's questioning face. "I just said that *this* isn't normal," she repeated more clearly.

"Your ability to fruitify?" Kip grinned. "You don't say."

"No, not me." She snorted. "Well, yes. Me. I'm clearly off-the-charts not normal. But I was talking about this pencil."

"What about it? It's a pencil. I mean, yeah, it's a Dimly pencil—"

"It sparkles." Daisy interrupted before Kip could launch into another art class lecture about the virtues of Dimly, shoving the pencil tip so close to his nose that Kip's eyes crossed.

Kip pried the pencil from her grasp and, without another mutter, bent over his own sketch pad, scribbling away first with the Dimly pencil and then a regular yellow HB pencil. After a moment, he spun the pad around and shoved it toward Daisy. There were two doodles on the page. Kip placed the regular pencil above one scribble and the Dimly pencil above the other. Daisy tried hard not to be annoyed by the fact that even Kip's scribbles looked like something out of Leonardo da Vinci's studio.

She leaned forward, peering closely at the page, comparing the two images while Kip waited. When, finally, she sat back and crossed her arms in smug satisfaction, he raised an eyebrow at her.

"Sparkly." She punctuated the word by pinning the Dimly sketch with her fingertip.

It was true. There was a faint but definite *glitter* to the marks the Dimly pencil had made. The lines shimmered when the page of the sketch pad caught the sun's rays.

"I bet if I tried to . . . uh . . . What was it again? Transmogrify . . . using a regular old pencil," Daisy said, "it wouldn't work."

"I'll take that bet!" Kip said. So he did. And she tried. And she *didn't*.

Daisy was right. No matter how hard she concentrated on a regular-pencil sketch of a simple goldfish, she didn't sprout so much as a wonky fin. Which was probably for the best, seeing as how they hadn't thought through the choice of subject matter before settling on goldfish and they were on dry land. If Kip hadn't been able to untransmogrify her, Daisy would've been one seriously gasping guppy. One seriously *ugly* gasping guppy.

"Wow, Kildare . . . that's . . . yeesh."

"Yup. I'm a prodigy, I tell you." She threw the pencil back on the table in disgust.

"Okay, okay." Kip tried not to wince looking at the hideous sketch. "Let's not get frustrated here."

"Easy for you to say."

"Look." He flipped over the page, mercifully hiding the doodle, and handed her the Dimly pencil. "Try this one. And maybe let's try an easier subject."

"How hard is a goldfish to draw?!" Daisy spluttered. "I mean, for someone who *can* draw."

"Try a mouse. You know, like, draw an oval, a

squiggle for a tail, a couple of dots for eyes, two little half-circle ears and some whiskers!" As he described the process, Kip demonstrated with Daisy's discarded HB. The result was almost lifelike.

Daisy sighed and rolled her eyes, held up the Dimly pencil, stuck her tongue out the side of her mouth and concentrated on the page in front of her with laser-like focus. She could feel her forehead tighten in a knot between her brows with the first tentative lines she drew.

She pressed the pencil to paper. The marks grew darker, more assured. Not any more aesthetically pleasing — it still looked like a mess of pencil squiggles — but they were *Dimly* pencil squiggles.

Daisy felt a tiny, tingly *zot*, like a static shock, in her fingertips. Then a stronger jolt, like touching an electric fence, running up her arm. Then a bolt of lightning hit her, or at least that's what it felt like, and she heard a loud *zzZAP!* The odour of burnt hair assailed her nose. Her really . . . *twitchy* . . . nose . . .

It was, she realized, exactly what she'd felt during the pineapple incident. Except for the nose-twitching part. Not having had a nose that time.

"Gleep?" she said, aiming the plaintive noise at Kip, who was staring in open-mouthed astonishment. Daisy had to tilt her head from side to side to focus on him properly. Without taking his eyes off her, Kip reached into his knapsack and pulled out one of the little stand-up mirrors the art students used on self-portrait day. He plunked it down in front of Daisy on the picnic table. It took her a second to focus on the reflected image, but when she did . . .

"GLEEP!" she exclaimed. Then took off running.

Okay, "running" might be a relative term. Daisy's uneven legs — all *four* of 'em — whirred and gangled, sticking out at odd angles and giving her a side-to-side, rolly-jumpy gait. Her crooked coat-hanger tail, which under normal rodent circumstances would have provided a counterbalance, whipped and flailed, occasionally spinning Daisy in a barrel roll before she could right herself.

As to exactly where Daisy was going, she wasn't sure. But she *was* sure she was freaked out. And freaking out demanded physical exertion. So she "ran" down the path to the beach and straight (straight*ish*) toward a pack of campers happily toasting s'mores over a blazing campfire.

Talk about freak-outs!

CHAPTER 12

RODENTS, AHOY!

"Giant rat!"

"Giant *mutant* rat!"

"Rabies!"

"Mange!"

"Fleas!"

Gerald looked over his shoulder, wondering what all the kerfuffle was about. It was s'mores day, an Art Camp tradition. Between sketching and painting and sculpting, campers headed down to the beach to toast the gooey goodies over bonfires. The lure of graham-cracker-marshmallow-chocolatey yumminess was too much for Gerald to ignore. Rats have very sensitive sniffers. Even three levels down in the Cryptolair, his nose had been twitching madly all day. Finally, like every year, he gave in to the urge to go to the beach and pilfer a batch of freshly fired s'mores.

He'd even stripped off his little white lab coat to travel incognito as a regular rat. S'mores might be the only thing that Gerald was willing to sacrifice his dignity — and risk catching a chill — over. Not that he expected to be spotted, of course. Gerald prided himself on his exceptionally stealthy sneaking. So he was rather surprised when people started howling about a rat on the beach.

He was even more surprised to discover that it wasn't *him* they were howling about! The rat that scurried by him in that moment was, well, rat*ish*, he supposed. It had all the various parts that went into the physical composition of a rodent, but they were all off-sized and in the wrong places.

The thing was strange. Hideous. Kind of fantastic! Gerald whipped out his custom-made, mad-scientist-built, rodent-minion-sized comm device (okay, it was basically just a tiny smart phone) and hit the *viz-uplink* (basically just the video call) button.

"Gav! Hey, Gav! Hey!" Gerald hiss-squeaked into the device, pointing the camera lens at the freaky, freaked-out critter bounding awkwardly from beach towel to log to shrub to water's edge and back again. "I think I got one!"

Dr. Gavin Bafflegab's face fizzled into view on the tiny screen. "It's *Doctor* Bafflegab, Gerald," he said in a tone that was half weary irritation and half irritated weariness. "Protocol is critical in the scientific commu—"

"Whateverdoctorbafflegabnevermindthatnow!" Gerald interrupted, blasting past the standard protocol lecture with an impressive lack of protocol. "I GOT ONE!"

Bafflegab blinked. "Got one *what*, Gerald?"

"A crypto! A cryptid! A . . . a . . . Got! One!"

The irritated irritation look returned in full force. "Don't be droll, Gerald—"

"LOOK!"

Gerald hit the reverse-camera button and pointed the device at the other "rat." The creature had bounded over to within about a metre of where Gerald was hiding, and its weirdo features filled the screen.

The thing made a sound like *gleep*, looking right into the camera (with one eye, anyway) before spinning around to awkwardly scramble away in the direction of the cabins. Gerald kept the bizarro thing in his viewfinder until it disappeared around the corner of the Common Cabin — the main gathering place for campers to play board games or do singalongs on days when the weather was too messy to spend outside.

"Follow that critter!"

His phone was yelling at him, Gerald realized. "Oh! Er, right! Bye!" Gerald hung up and took off running as fast as his little feet would carry him, his dreams of pilfered s'mores left far behind.

What Gerald, in his frantic pursuit, failed to notice — indeed, what everyone at the beach missed in the panicky confusion — were the ripples and splash on the surface of Lake Okanagan and the dark, sinewy shape moving beneath. They also collectively overlooked the tall, hairy shadow lurking beneath the pine trees, then disappearing moments later. And no one in the chaotic scramble to avoid the mangy-rabid mutant rat thing even thought to glance skyward when an oddly rabbit-shaped winged shadow floated over the beach, vanishing behind the distant hills.

The Art Camp bulletin boards had notices up within the hour warning campers not to feed the "whatever-it-is." The camp administration had discreetly laid out traps (humane ones) about an hour after that. Unfortunately, the only thing they managed to catch all afternoon was Percy the rescue marmot. Repeatedly.

Mostly because Percy liked cages. And attention. And the stale cherry danishes used to bait the traps.

Of course, Percy wasn't the only reason the traps failed to nab the fugitive "whatever-it-is." Because, with the help of Kip's trusty Pink Pearl eraser, it had become a "whatever-it-*was*." Within minutes of having unwittingly terrorized a beach full of campers, Daisy had already successfully untransmogrified. But that brief, bizarre appearance had been enough to crank the camp counsellors up to high alert. The last thing the camp needed was for word to get out to parents that there was some kind of rodent trouble. And the administrators weren't the only ones determined to catch the creepy critter that had run amok.

Back at the Cryptolair, Gerald paused playback on his comm device. Then he reversed and slow-mo-ed through the digital footage for the eighteenth time, freeze-framing and zooming in on the moment the cryptid had rounded the corner of the Common Cabin and vanished from sight.

"There!" he muttered, stabbing at the screen with one pointy toe. "There's something else. No! Some*one* else!" Someone with a bucket. And a net. And . . . a sketchbook?

It was barely more than a brief, blurry flash of movement, but it seemed that, in the second before the cryptid disappeared from view, someone had appeared to capture the thing using the bucket and net.

"Huh," Gerald muttered. "It seems we have some unexpected competition in the cryptid-capturing department." And *that* would never do. He sat there pondering his next move, his tiny claws drumming on the comm device screen.

He ran the clip again, this time with the volume turned all the way up. There was the cacophony of screams and screeches from the panicked campers, and the sound of flip-flops and sneakers pounding up and down the paths. Gerald hooked his device up to one of the Cryptolair's computers and ran it through a noise-filtering program. And there it was. Faintly but distinctly, a lone voice called out: "Kildare!" And then, "Daaaaisyyyyy . . ."

It faded into the distance at about the same time as the shadowy bucket-and-net figure and the cryptid did. Or rather, Gerald thought, the "cryptid." He made little tiny air quotes with his front toes as he mentally put the quotation marks around the word. Something had stirred in the back of his genius-rat brain. Kildare. Daisy Kildare.

He suddenly remembered where he'd heard that name before! Daisy Kildare, Gerald knew, was *not* a cryptid. But she *was* one of Dr. Fassbinder's reidium subjects. The one that got away . . . Gerald's nose twitched furiously with glee.

This was certainly an unexpected development — and one that could be *verrry* valuable at that! But Gerald was going to have to be cagey about when, or even *if*, he would reveal his discovery. And to whom. Bafflegab? The Boss? Maybe even Fassbinder! *No*, not him. Department C, the government bureau responsible for all things Boredom Institute, was flat broke. Even if Gerald dangled the Kildare girl for ransom, they'd probably just try to pay him off in cheese wheels.

The Boss, on the other hand, didn't have much money to speak of either — but what she *did* have were aspirations of world domination. Which, if successful, would mean money. Bafflegab, on the *other* other hand, had money. Tons of it, from his successful grant applications. But he was so obsessively wrapped up in his mythical-monster hunting that he lacked vision. Gerald had vision. And patience.

That was it, he decided. He'd wait, bide his time, and see how things shook out before he made his move and revealed his secret.

Or rather, Daisy Kildare's secret.

CHAPTER 13

DOODLE TUTOR TOODLE-OO

"Please take the bucket off my head."

Kip was laughing so hard he barely heard Daisy's muffled request. To be fair, the whole situation was pretty hilarious. After all the scurrying and scrabbling, Kip had successfully prodded Sketchy-Daisy into a bucket trap. (He'd had a lot of practice with that sort of thing, from every time Percy escaped the yard.) While she was trapped under the bucket, he'd gotten to work with the eraser. Moments later, ta-dah! Reverse transmogrification!

Still chortling, Kip grabbed hold with both hands and gave the bucket a mighty tug. It popped off Daisy's head, and the momentum propelled him backwards. He tripped over a tree root but, much to his — and

Daisy's — surprise, managed to execute a pretty decent shoulder roll in recovery.

"Nice," Daisy said, with a tilt of her head.

"Thanks!" Kip said, wiping tears of laughter from his eyes as he pulled Daisy's hat out of his knapsack and handed it over.

Daisy snatched it from his hand and plopped it back on her head with a grumbled *harumph*. It didn't fit much better than the bucket had because her hair *still* hadn't reverted back to her natural waves. Daisy was beginning to suspect that as long as the birthday card self-portrait existed somewhere, it wasn't about to unsproing. When things got back to normal she was going to have to shoot Jess a message and ask her to take an eraser to that sketch.

But Daisy had more important things to worry about at the moment.

"Check it out, Kildare." Kip was shaking his head, having regained his composure. Mostly. "This is *so* cool!" He held up his phone, swiping through the pictures he'd managed to take as he chased Sketchy-Daisy all over the camp. "You're, like, a human 3-D printer!"

"Yeah." Daisy rolled her eyes and looked at the pictures. "With a short circuit."

"All you need is a few drawing lessons," Kip said. "Look, I'll convince my mom that you need a tutor."

"A tutor?"

"Yeah — a tutor!" Kip pointed at himself. "That'll get you out of regular classes, and we'll be able to work on your technique tomorrow, okay? I checked your schedule for today — you've only got one other session this afternoon and that's abstract fingerpainting. Even you can't screw that up."

Daisy raised an eyebrow at him from beneath the brim of her hat.

"Um. Heh. You know what I mean. Tomorrow, bright and early, we'll meet back here and get started. Deal?" He thrust out his hand.

"Deal." Daisy reluctantly shook on it.

That afternoon's fingerpainting class was gloriously uneventful. And then it was singalongs that evening, sitting around a campfire on the beach as vigilant counsellors stood guard with butterfly nets reinforced with duct tape, just in case the "whatever-it-is" made an appearance.

Daisy was understandably distracted by the events of the day. So it wasn't really her fault that she failed to notice the glowing eyes in the trees beyond the firelight. If she had, she might have noticed that they were staring. Right. At. Her.

CHAPTER 14

ANOTHER DAY, ANOTHER DOODLE

"Way better!" Kip exclaimed the next morning as Daisy untransmogrified into her regular Daisy form. "I could tell which end was the front and which was the back this time . . ." He brushed the last of the pink eraser shreds from the now-blank page of Daisy's sketch pad.

"You really think so?" Daisy untangled herself and stood, blowing a corkscrew strand of hair from her face. "You're not just saying that to make me feel better?"

"*Pff.*" Kip waved away her concerns. "Of course not. Here, let's try something a little different—"

"Kip?" Daisy frowned. "Why are you doing this? I mean — thanks! — but . . . why?"

"Are you kidding?" Kip goggled at her. "You know

this is all kinds of amazing, right? I mean, why do I run around trying to leap tall buildings, or really short buildings, y'know? Dumpsters and such, anyway? I mean, why do you think?"

Daisy blinked at him. He snorted, as if the answer was obvious and she just wasn't thinking the whole thing through. "It's a desire to be *different*, Kildare!" he said. "Special. And if I can't be the superhero — 'cause that's clearly *you* — then I can at least aspire to be one heck of a sidekick, right?"

"Uh, right. I mean, I guess?"

"Besides," Kip continued, "you need me to erase your sketchies. Also, I think you're cool."

"I think you're cool too."

"Okay, okay." He rolled his eyes. "Group hug and all that. Now back to work!"

He beckoned Daisy to grab her sketch pad and follow him. Kip led her down an overgrown path to a sheltered bit of Lake Okanagan shoreline where the water formed a shallow, clear pool. They crouched there, watching the minnows darting.

"Fish," Kip said, pointing at the little silver critters. "Why don't you try a fish again? Only this time nearer water, in case you're successful — which you will be!"

"I dunno." Daisy eyed the sparkling lake water warily. Only a few metres from shore it turned a deep shade of blue. "What if I run into that Ogopogo guy everyone's always talking about? Heh . . ." She said it jokingly, but really she was far more worried about whether, in a transmogrified state, she could actually breathe underwater without drowning.

"Yeah." Kip shook his head. "No. No using monsters as an excuse. Oggy's no more real than Bigfoot is. The only thing you have to worry about around here as far as that goes is running into the crazy dude who lives in the forest and claims to be a monster hunter."

"Is that true?" Daisy glanced past him at the cool green depths of the shadowy forest. "A couple of the girls in my cabin were talking about that last night."

"He's been out there for years. Claims to be a 'scientist,' but all the locals know he's just some nutty English dude. He's harmless. And he hasn't caught a thing in ten years." Kip brandished the Pink Pearl eraser between them. "Now quit stalling, Kildare. If I lose sight of you once you're in the water, I'll count to twenty and then I'll erase the sketchy. Er . . . you *can* swim, right?"

"Yeah." Daisy nodded. "But I'm leaving my hat on dry land."

Daisy dipped a toe into the chilly lake water and shivered. With cold, sure, but maybe with a little excitement too. She clutched her Dimly pencil — less tightly than she had been initially, thanks to Kip's tutoring — and concentrated. She drew her first fishy outline faintly, with light, feathery strokes of the pencil — also thanks to Kip's instructions — then retraced the lines that seemed to be in the right place and redrew the ones that seemed wildly off-kilter. She could feel the now-familiar furrows appear between her eyebrows and the tip of her tongue peek out from the corner of her mouth.

Slowly, gradually something *vaguely* fishy appeared on the page. There was a tingle, a *ZZOooOOTtTT*!! And with a splash, Daisy found herself submerged, flipping her (mismatched) fins and swimming in wobbly little circles! And *breathing*! It was weird and a little bit wonderful because it felt almost like breathing air, only cooler and wetter, and she could feel the water flowing through her gills!

Thank goodness I remembered to draw gills! she thought.

She did a little loop-the-loop that took her into deeper water and was dazzled by the light reflecting on the surface above her. She blinked her (pretty wonky) fish eyes but that just messed with her sense of which way was up. Disoriented, Daisy started swimming down when she meant to swim up and back toward Kip and the beach. Strands of seaweed drifted past her face, growing into a thick underwater forest as she went deeper. Then suddenly the green strands parted and Daisy could see clearly.

Which made it really hard to ignore the giant sea serpent swimming past, *right* in front of her.

Daisy opened her mouth to scream and an explosion of bubbles enveloped her face, obscuring her vision — which was back to 20/20, because *she* was back to being human! She thrashed around, flailing the arms and legs that had sprouted in place of the fins she'd had only moments earlier. It churned the water, stirring up clouds of silt from the bottom and turning everything murky. Daisy kicked hard and shot upward. Her head broke the surface of the lake and she splashed and gasped, trying to shake the tangle of hair from her eyes.

She could hear Kip calling her name frantically from the shore and she spun in a circle, treading water, until she saw him waving, the eraser clutched in his fist. She dog-paddled over and clambered onto the little stretch of beach.

"Holy moly, Kildare!" Kip gasped. "For a minute there, I thought Ogopogo got you!"

"For a minute, so did I!" she said.

"Wait. What?" Kip blinked. "I was kidding. I just thought you drowned or something."

"What? No! There was a monster!" She flailed her arms at the serene lake. "A serpent sea! I mean, a sea serpent! Out there. The Pogogogo!"

"Ogopogo."

"Yes!"

"No."

"What?"

Kip grabbed Daisy by the shoulders and shook her a little. "It's a myth, Kildare. I mean, it's a *cool* myth, but there's no such thing!"

"But . . . but . . . I saw . . . Um. Something."

"Think for a second," Kip reasoned. "You were underwater. Maybe a little disoriented. Seeing everything through a fish-eye lens. Two of them. Literally. It was probably just a big old trout. Or a perch. Or a sunken log."

Daisy was starting to question what she'd seen herself. It *had* been dark. And weedy. And—

"Did you hear that?" She whipped her head around at a sound that came, not from the lake, but from the trees.

"Hear what?" Kip asked.

"Like . . . a twig snapping."

"Oh, yeah, that." He shrugged. "It sounded like a twig snapping. Are you hungry?"

"I really am." She nodded enthusiastically. "All this transmogrifying sure works up an appetite!"

Daisy shrugged off the lingering sense of unease at the thought of the sea serpent. Kip was right. If such a thing did exist, someone surely would have produced indisputable proof by now. Right . . . ? It wasn't exactly small. As they headed back for lunch, Daisy glanced over her shoulder and thought she saw the flick of a tail fin out in the middle of the lake.

"Okay. Myth. But," she murmured as she walked, "if *I'm* real, who's to say a sea monster is *that* big of a stretch?"

CHAPTER 15

OPERATION CUNNING PLAN

"Stupid snappy twigs," Gerald muttered to himself as he scurried back to the Cryptolair's hidden entrance. "Almost gave me away . . ."

Gerald had ditched his naked-rat disguise (*non-disguise*, really) for a more reconnaissance ensemble. He wore head-to-toe camouflage — jacket, pants, green-and-black face paint (he was going to have a heck of a time washing it out of his fur later) and little black combat boots. S'mores pilfering was one thing, but this? *This* was serious business.

And Gerald had, over the course of the afternoon, gathered some serious intel. Intel that he would use to his very best advantage. Once he knew what he was looking for, tracking down his quarry had proved to be a piece of cake. First, he'd used his comm device to remotely hack into the database back at the Boredom Institute and download the most recent picture of Daisy Kildare. He'd been keeping up on Doc Fassbinder's annual testing of the Dimly kids and knew that she and her mother had skipped town and disappeared just over a year ago, so the picture was a little out of date, but it did the trick.

A different, and rather questionable, hairdo almost fooled him, but eventually he spotted Daisy among the campers, hanging out with some kid who seemed unable to walk ten steps without tripping over his own sneakers. Gerald had followed them to a remote spot on the beach. And what he'd learned had pasted an Eeeeevil grin on his furry little mug that was still there as he scampered through the undergrowth.

At the base of a soaring pine tree split by lightning sometime in the distant past, he scrambled around the side of a fake rock and, hidden by a fake juniper bush, gave a little jump to hit the *down* button on an elevator call panel. It was a special rodent-height one that had been installed since he'd joined Team Crypto, but it was still a little high for him to reach without the extra leap.

A widening crack, like a seam of light, appeared in the rock, and the hidden elevator doors slid open.

Gerald stepped inside the plushly decorated cab and braced himself as the high-speed elevator lurched and the floor dropped out from under his feet. Gerald swallowed hard against the momentary motion sickness as the cab came to a bumpy stop and the doors opened with a hiss.

He trotted through the maze of metallic underground corridors like a mouse in search of a cheese reward. (Ugh, cheese! Mice! Ugh!) Gerald's comm device, full of priceless digital video, was safely stowed in one of the many pockets of his camo cargo pants. He was almost bursting with excitement as he entered the Cryptolair's command centre.

"Gav! Gav!" he squeaked. "You're NOT going to believe this . . ."

Bafflegab didn't even bother with the lecture on protocol, greedily making grabby hands for the comm device. Gerald bypassed Baffle's flailing digits and scrambled onto a gleaming chrome countertop in front of a digital playback unit. He unspooled a cable, plugged in the device and hit *play*. Then he sat back and watched as Dr. Bafflegab's jaw hit the floor.

Half an hour — and many, *many* replays — later, the cryptozoologist sat in his chair digesting the impossible, yet utterly plausible, hypothesis offered up by his genius rodent assistant. Gerald waited patiently.

"You're absolutely certain Daisy Kildare is the name of the girl from Fassbinder's research?" Bafflegab asked finally.

"Does a Pianvian grandma love her Splotnik?" Gerald answered.

"Do you know what this means?" the cryptozoologist said, a greasy grin sliding across his face.

Gerald did know.

That was why in the end, he'd decided to divulge his intel to Bafflegab. The Boss was The Big Bad. But Baffles was something else. Something useful: a self-deluded egomaniac. Gerald had always suspected that Bafflegab's fascination with cryptozoology was not the noble pursuit he wanted everyone to believe. Maybe it was fame, notoriety or plain old greed that drove him, but dangling the prospect of one of the reidium kids seemed every bit as tantalizing to Bafflegab as a real live Yeti capture.

Whatever the case, Bafflegab was smart enough to keep the discovery from The Boss for the moment — at least until he had an actual bargaining chip in his hot little hands. And dumb enough not to realize that he was being manipulated by a rat.

Just then a red light on the console lit up — The Boss's direct line.

"Hold my calls, Gerald," Bafflegab said with a grin.

Gerald pressed the *hold* button without answering. Then he and Bafflegab shared a good ol' fashioned Eeeeevil laugh.

"Richrichrich. I'm rich! Richity richity rich rich rich," Bafflegab sang, dancing a little jig at the thought of the obscene amounts of wealth.

"Hee hee hee," he chortled. "The Boss will pay handsomely for such a marvellous acquisition!" He rubbed his greedy mitts together. "And if she won't, someone else will! All we have to do is catch that ridiculous girl and entice her to use her power for us."

Gerald knew that by "entice" Bafflegab actually meant "threaten," but he ignored the uneasy twist of guilt in his stomach.

"The sketch pad is the key," he reminded Bafflegab as he finished stuffing a rope net into a canvas bag. "And the pencil."

"Right." Bafflegab nodded. "If we don't have those, we don't have anything."

"Which means we have to kidnap the clumsy kid too."

"Or trick him into handing over the goods." Bafflegab let loose with another round of nefarious chuckles. "Now be a good chap, Gerald. Put that genius rodent brain of yours to work and come up with a cunning plan, won't you?"

Gerald rolled his beady little eyes and muttered to himself. Why didn't Gav put his *own* genius brain to work? *Mutter mutter.* Because, oh yeah, he didn't *have* a genius brain . . .

Soon Gerald and Bafflegab were going all out preparing traps. Traps that, in the past, had been set with the intention of catching a cryptid or two, and which had remained entirely empty for all that time. But now that Gerald knew where to find Daisy Kildare, he was certain he could set a trap that would catch her, easy as pie. After all, Daisy herself had said that transmogrifying made her hungry.

They hid an assortment of traps, big and small, in the undergrowth beside the paths to where Daisy and

Kip had been having their sketching sessions. They baited them with goodies that might entice a hungry, transmogrified creature-girl.

And then they waited. And waited. And waited . . .

And Percy the rescue marmot escaped from his cabin — again — and struck out into the woods in search of something he'd smelled through a crack in the window: cherry danishes. His favourite.

ABSTRACTS

"But, Mom—"

"Stay out of this, Kipper." Mrs. Winklehorn shot a glare at Kip before turning a stern but understanding gaze back on Daisy. While Kip and Daisy had been conducting their goldfish experiment, they'd lost track of time and hadn't realized that Daisy had missed the one block of class that day that wasn't devoted to her "tutorial" sessions with Kip.

"Now, Daisy," Kip's mom continued with her lecture, "it's just not appropriate for you to treat Art Camp as some kind of goof-off holiday."

"Believe me, Mrs. W.," Daisy said, "I'm not."

"Well then how do you explain skipping your self-portrait session?"

Daisy shuddered, remembering her very first attempt at such a thing, and one hand crept toward her hair. "I don't belong in a class like that! I'm just . . . I can't do what those kids can do."

"Nonsense," Mrs. Winklehorn *tsked*. "You're *here*, aren't you? Let me see your sketch pad."

Daisy reluctantly handed it over. The only thing on the pages of the pad that hadn't been erased by Kip was the regular HB pencil sketch Daisy had done of the goldfish — the one that *hadn't* transmogrified her. Mrs. Winklehorn flipped to that page and recoiled in horror.

"Gah!" she exclaimed. "What *is* that?!"

"Goldfish," Daisy said glumly. "See?"

"How on earth did you even get *into* Art Camp, dear?" Mrs. Winklehorn asked, mystified. "There's an entrance portfolio exam and—"

"*You* signed me up," Daisy said. "With a full scholarship. On the merits of a birthday-card doodle."

"Oh. Right. I seem to remember . . . I . . . Oh dear." Kip's mom grimaced. "I suppose the responsibility is mine, then. But I don't know what we're going to do about the gala exhibit. Every student has to have something worthy to put on display at the final barbecue and show!"

"Um, well, Kip *has* been tutoring me . . ."

"She's gotten way better!" he chimed in.

The look on Mrs. Winklehorn's face expressed just how unlikely she thought it was that would improve Daisy's chances at producing a show-worthy piece.

"She's not lying," Kip said. "We haven't been goofing around, Mom. I really *have* been tutoring her. She's got, uh, talent. It's just . . . *unusual* talent. It's hard to explain. Really abstract stuff."

"*Really* abstract." Daisy nodded solemnly.

Kip's mom stared at him through narrowed eyes. "Is this all part of your avant-garde project or something, Kip?" she asked.

"Uh. Yes . . . ?" Kip had actually forgotten what he'd told his mom about the ugly pineapple thing. But it made for a brilliant cover — one that his mom herself had just provided! "Yes! That's exactly it. I call it *Ugly So Ugly It's Beautiful*. Daisy is, um, my collaborator. We're collaborating. And it's going to be *the* next big thing on the international art scene, I guarantee it! New York galleries will be calling non-stop!"

"Well, far be it from me to stifle creativity." Mrs. Winklehorn glanced again at the goldfish sketch and shuddered. "I just don't see it, but . . ."

Kip elbowed Daisy and together they pasted on the best, brightest, most *artiste* smiles they could muster.

"All right." Mrs. Winklehorn finally gave in and

threw up her hands. "Daisy, you can have a special exemption from all your regular sessions — so long as Kip agrees to keep tutoring you on an individual project basis. *But* you two had better come up with something *spectacular* by the end of Camp. Or else."

"We will!" Kip nodded enthusiastically.

"Oh, totally." Daisy swallowed nervously.

Mrs. Winklehorn picked up the sketch pad by its corner as if the thing was radioactive (which it probably was, a bit) and handed it back to Daisy. She shooed the two of them out of her office, and they made a run for it before she changed her mind. But when they got back to the Winklehorn cabin, their relief at getting let off the hook — at least until the barbecue banquet 'n' show — soon vanished, obliterated by the note Kip found propped against a bowl of fruit on the counter.

"What is it?" Daisy asked, watching Kip as he read the note.

Kip felt the blood draining from his face as he read the last sentence on the paper. Wordlessly, he handed it over. Daisy read it for herself. Then she did something Kip hadn't seen her do before.

Daisy Kildare got angry.

CHAPTER 17

CRITTER TRAPS

While Daisy and Kip were busy getting lectured by Kip's mom, Bafflegab and Gerald were busy setting traps. And when the proximity alarm went off on one of them, sending a signal to Gerald's comm device (he really was a genius, and very good at inventing stuff), the two of them hurried to the freshly sprung trap.

When they got close, Gerald peered through a set of tiny high-powered binoculars to see what they'd nabbed, hoping it wasn't just one of the local chipmunks. A rope net hung from a tree branch, and there was definitely something inside. Something furry. He adjusted the focus for a better view and . . .

"Gah!" he exclaimed, fumbling the binoculars and dropping them.

"What?" Bafflegab grabbed for them, putting them up to the bridge of his nose and crossing his eyes so he could look through the tiny eyeholes. "What is — GAH!"

"Told you."

"That thing! What is it?" He adjusted the tiny focus wheel. "Only that Kildare girl could draw something like this — it must be her! Let's go get it!"

They approached and Gerald scampered up the tree to gnaw through the rope that suspended the net. When it fell to the ground with a *thump-squeak!* he and Bafflegab pounced on the occupant with a canvas bag. Then they stuffed the squirming bag into a kitty carrier and lugged the whole shebang back to the Cryptolair.

It was only when they dumped the carrier out on the floor of one of the cells that had been specially built (but, of course, never occupied) to house a cryptid that they realized the extent of their mistake. As wonky as Percy was — and Bafflegab made sure to make his opinions loudly known on that — he was definitely not of supernatural origin. Nowhere *near* as bizarre-looking as the creatures Daisy's pencil conjured, nor as diabolically useful. He was, upon close inspection, just a run-of-the-mill, three-legged, one-eyed, wonky-eared rescue marmot.

It was probably a good thing Percy didn't have an ego to bruise, because all of that talk might have hurt his little marmot feelings. As it was, the insults just rolled off his scraggly back. And really, Percy had nothing to be ashamed of. He made a break for the open cell door and was surprisingly fast and agile on his three little legs, tucking and rolling and leaping and diving in ways that would make Kip's parkour-loving heart soar.

The feisty little critter might have gotten away clean if it wasn't for his one weakness. Not his lack of leg, or his missing eye, or his wonky ears. No, no. It was his weakness for *pastries* that did him in. He was on the very threshold of escape when Gerald fished a slightly melted spare apricot danish from the knapsack that had held the trap supplies and fastball-pitched the pastry into the open kitty carrier . . . and Percy dove right back in after it!

Bafflegab slammed the cage shut, and the cell went silent. Except, of course, for the adorable sound of munching marmot murmles.

"Useless!" Bafflegab spat, furious at the turn of events. "It's not the reidium girl. It's not even a blasted cryptid!"

"It's not a wild animal either," Gerald said, peering through the carrier door. "It's just that awkward kid's rescue pet."

Bafflegab's eyes narrowed. "Hmm . . ." he murmured, scratching his chin in thought, a tiny glint of evil sparking in his gaze. "Pet . . ." He turned to look over his shoulder and saw that Gerald had grabbed the cage's bungee cord in his teeth and was dragging the carrier out of the cell and into the corridor.

"I'll just take the creature back outside," Gerald said through a mouthful of bungee, heading toward the hydraulic lift that led to the surface, "and let it go—"

"*Where* are you going with that cage?"

The tone of the question stopped him cold. Gerald spat out the cord and sat back on his haunches, blinking up at Bafflegab. "You just said the animal was of no use to us."

"I said nothing of the kind."

"Actually, you did." Gerald shook his head. "You said 'useless.' That means of no use."

"That's not what I meant."

"But—"

"There's something I've come to understand after all my years of cryptozoology, Gerald." The glint in Bafflegab's eye grew to a gleam. "And that's the science of animal behaviour. *Especially* when it comes to humans and hard-luck cases. People love sob stories when it comes to animals." He shifted his tone to a mocking singsong. "Poor lonely Nessie! Leave Bigfoot alone! That bloodthirsty chupacabra probably just needs a hug!"

A shiver ran up Gerald's spine. He could see where this was going and, nefarious or not, he didn't like it. No siree, he didn't like it one bit. Gerald may have considered himself to be first-rate Eeeeevil, but the reality was that he was just the smartest rat in the room — almost any room, especially ones occupied by the likes of Gavin Bafflegab — and he resented the lack of recognition for his superior intellect. What he'd told himself all along was an affinity for Eeeeevil-doing was really just a case of hurt feelings. Bafflegab was a different story. And Gerald was just beginning to realize it.

"In *this* instance," Bafflegab continued, shifting back to his regular snooty accent, "the hard-luck case is Exhibit A: a much-doted-on mutt of a rescue pet. Or, as I prefer to call such a creature . . . 'bait.'"

Then he laughed an actual "Mwuah-hah-hah-ha-haaa" Eeeeevil laugh and pulled out a stack of magazines and a pair of scissors, shoving them in front of Gerald.

CHAPTER 18

FOLLOW THAT DOG!

Daisy's knuckles went white as she finished reading the ransom note and handed it back to Kip.

"Percy's been kidnapped." Kip's voice was a strangled whisper. "What am I going to do? He's my best pal! I'm responsible for him—"

"Kip . . . Kip!" Daisy grabbed him by the shoulder and squeezed until he looked her in the eyes. Then she said, "Where's my sketch pad?"

"I don't understand this. Why would someone want to kidnap Percy? He's barely even housebroken! He smells terrible!"

"Show me the note again."

Kip handed it over. It was composed of mismatched letters cut from various magazine ads.

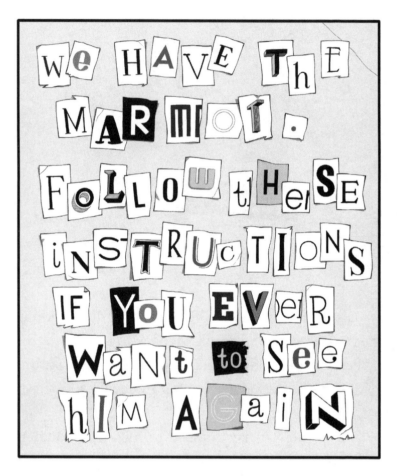

We have the marmot. Follow these instructions if you ever want to see him again

The instructions were typed out on the other side: *Take the overgrown path beyond the unused firepits. Walk for ten minutes (until you come to a pleasant clearing). Stop. Wait. Tell no one! Bring the girl and her art supplies. Just do it. No questions!*

"Do you think it's one of the other campers?" Daisy asked, mystified. "Somebody jealous of your talent?

Somebody other than me, I mean . . ."

Kip shook his head in despair. "Even the First Years could put together a better-looking ransom collage than this."

It was pretty sloppy, Daisy had to agree. Plus, it didn't really make all that much sense. Why did *she* have to go along? Why did she have to bring her art stuff? What kind of goofy ransom instructions were those, anyway? Whatever. The kidnappers were about to be disappointed. Daisy had never been very good at following orders.

"Come on," she said, and motioned for Kip to follow her — in the *opposite* direction of the overgrown path beyond the unused firepits. Once they were into the forest and far enough away from the cabins to be hidden from sight, Daisy busted out her sketch pad and Dimly pencil. She cleared her mind, centred her breathing, wiggled her fingers, rolled her shoulders, cracked her knuckles . . .

And froze.

"What?" Kip asked, gasping and out of breath because he'd successfully leap frogged over three boulders and side-jumped another using a tree stump as a launch — all without even *realizing* it. "What's wrong?"

The pencil hovered over the sketch pad page, which

was as blank as Daisy's imagination in that moment. Perhaps she'd cleared her mind just a bit *too* much.

"I . . . I can't." She looked up at Kip, her eyes filled with stark panic. "I was going to draw something cool to turn into to help us rescue Percy—"

"That's a great idea!"

"But I can't think of anything to *draw!*" she wailed. "I . . . I've got artist's block. Which would only make any sense whatsoever if I was an actual artist!"

"Daisy—"

"The truth is, I suck at drawing, Kip!" Daisy shook her head angrily. "And even if I *do* get something down on the page, it'll probably be just another monster. A *useless* monster! Percy's been petnapped and I'm no help to you at all!"

"Hey, hey," Kip said, trying to calm her. "You *are* an artist, Daisy Kildare! You might be the most amazing artist I've ever met. Critics talk about making a piece of art come alive, but you? You actually *do* that!"

"I . . . I do?"

"You do." He plucked the pencil from where she'd dropped it in a pile of pine needles and held it in front of her face. "Now draw!"

Daisy reached for the pencil. She turned back to the empty, gleaming-white page and concentrated. She let her mind go blank again, then let it fill back up with whatever it felt like. And then she started to scribble. Line by squiggly line, she drew a picture of . . . of . . . of a bloodhound! Yes!

As a tracking dog, Sketchy-Daisy could sniff out quarry from great distances over almost any kind of terrain. And she'd drawn the pup's nose extra large, just so she'd have no trouble whatsoever sniffing out Percy's trail. Which, in hindsight, might have been a bit of overkill. The moment after she transmogrified, Daisy was so overwhelmed she let out a *Woof!* — only her nose was so big it came out as more of a *Bloof!* — and then she toppled forward, the weight of her doggy snout overbalancing her head and causing her to tip.

But as she righted herself, she was amazed in a doggy kind of way at all the things she could actually smell! Some of them she wished she couldn't, but she pushed those things to the back of her doggy awareness.

Kip held the ransom note in front of her face, and she sniffed and snuffled the page and was overcome with a single bloodhound thought: *RAT.*

"Good girl!" Kip cheered as she spun and bounded into the underbrush, following the scent of the rodent who'd written that note. "Right behind ya . . ."

As she loped along, Bloodhound-Daisy kept tripping on her uneven, too-long ears. But even that barely slowed her down. In short order, she turned off the marked footpath, scrambled through the undergrowth, and dove headfirst through a (fake!) juniper bush. Her doggy nose booped the slightly-higher-than-rat-level call button hidden there, and then her overlong floppy ears picked up the sound of an underground hydraulic hum. The (also fake!) rock in front of her cracked open and elevator doors slid aside.

"Holy moly," murmured Kip, who'd just managed to catch up with her.

Together they stepped inside the elevator and pressed the button marked *down.* After a brief barfy-feeling plummet, the doors opened and Kip and Bloodhound-Daisy stepped cautiously out.

The place — whatever it was — was deserted, with corridors stretching out in two directions. The gentle illumination of recessed lighting was complemented by a wavering greenish-blue glow from windows, like aquarium viewing portholes, spaced evenly along the corridor ceiling and walls.

They were *under* Lake Okanagan.

"Whoa . . ." Kip breathed, looking around in awe. Then he turned to Daisy and asked, "Which way?"

"Wuf." Daisy wasn't sure. The whole place smelled of RAT to her nose, and the shiny, solid steel surfaces of the walls and floor made it hard to tell which smells were newer. She looked up at Kip and doggy-shrugged. So he flipped a coin.

Minutes later, Daisy and Kip approached a massive steel door at the end of their coin-toss-chosen corridor on silent feet. Well, silentish. Kip's sneakers squeaked a bit and Daisy's raggedly drawn claws clicked if she stepped the wrong way with her back feet. But they didn't set off any alarms — that they could tell — and seemed to pass unnoticed. Well, *almost* unnoticed . . .

As they passed one of the thick, round Plexiglas portholes set into the wall, neither Kip nor Daisy noticed the long, twisty shadow that zigzagged through the green-blue lake water beyond.

There was no handle or knob on the door, but Kip poked at a button panel set in the wall, and after a moment the steel slab slid open with a rusty hiss. The air from the room beyond had a musty scent to it, as if that door hadn't been opened in a long time. The room was lit, but not brightly.

"We alone?" Kip asked Daisy quietly.

"Snuff," she grunted, and padded inside.

"Are you sure you can't smell anyone else in here right now?" He followed, warily. "We're the only people here?"

Bloodhound-Daisy cocked her floppy-eared head from side to side. She wasn't entirely sure. She knew, instinctively, that Kip was the only *human* in that wing of the complex. Human smell was an entirely unique smell. And she also knew Percy was somewhere nearby. (Having spent a bit of time scritching his wonky ears after she'd reverted from her pineapple state, she was familiar with his rather signature aroma.) The RAT was nearby too. Well, nearbyish, anyway.

There were other smells as well. A whole smell soup that Daisy couldn't quite untangle fogged the air. Some of the scents were overpowering, and for a few dizzying moments, she wished she was Jess Flem — her friend from Dimly with allergies so hyperactive that she couldn't smell a skunk if it crawled up under her nose.

She sat down and looked up at Kip. "Huff," she huffed.

"Okay." He nodded in understanding. "I'm going to erase you now."

Daisy nodded back, her too-long ear flopping over her eyes and her too-long tongue flapping across her nose. Kip trotted behind a desk and opened the sketch pad to the sketchy-dog page. He dug around in Daisy's bag for the Pink Pearl eraser and got to work. A good solid minute of erasing . . . and *zZAPppOOWEee!!* Daisy was back, crouched on hands and knees.

"Well," rumbled a deep growling voice from behind her, "now that really is a neat trick."

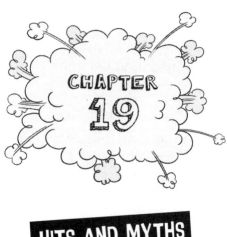

CHAPTER 19

HITS AND MYTHS

Kip's face registered a mix of wild astonishment and sheer terror.

Daisy stood and slowly turned around. Her bloodhound nose had been right on the money. There weren't any other humans in the vicinity. Daisy had never stopped to think that all those other smells she'd been smelling might have been something *other* than human. But the seven-foot-tall, enormously muscled creature covered in long shaggy red fur *definitely* fell into the non-human category. Daisy looked down at the floor where the massive thing was standing.

Huh, she thought, numb with shock. The non-human category had a subheading that read: "Bigfoot."

He stood in front of an open door that neither Daisy nor Kip had noticed. Beyond the threshold was another room with flickering dim lights, most likely powered by an auxiliary generator of some kind. But there was enough illumination to outline the beastly creature in an unearthly greenish glow. It was the very same creature that — along with the legendary sea serpent of the lake they were currently underneath — Kip had earlier managed to convince Daisy was nothing more than a myth.

"Stop right there!" Kip shouted, suddenly breaking free from his trancelike state.

Daisy turned to see him looking around wildly for something he could use as a weapon. He found a piece of lab equipment that looked like an unlit Bunsen burner and grabbed it, brandishing it high over his head.

"Step away from her you . . . you . . . uh . . ."

"The term you're searching for is probably 'sasquatch,'" the sasquatch said helpfully.

"Right!" Kip rebrandished the burner. "Uh. You . . . you . . . can . . ."

"Talk?" The broad, hairy face split into a snaggletoothed grin. "Yup. I can talk, all right. Better than *you* at the moment there, little buddy." The creature ambled forward on his truly *enormous* feet and extended a massive, long-fingered hand. "The guys call me Big Red."

Kip and Daisy, both raised to be polite in even the most astonishing of circumstances, shook hands with the sasquatch.

"The . . . um. The guys . . . ?" Daisy managed to ask.

"Well, the others." Big Red shrugged his mountainous shoulders. "Some of 'em are girls, of course. And most of 'em can't *really* talk — not in human words, anyway — so they just call me whatever 'Big Red' works out to in their own individual languages."

Daisy realized that Kip had gone silent, and she turned to see that he had drifted toward the entrance to the room beyond the door and was staring (politeness training only went so far, all things considered) at *another* cryptid. This one was standing in front of a fax machine in the far corner of the room, which was crammed with scientific and office equipment, and was almost an exact copy of Big Red, only with snow-white fur.

"Who's that guy?" Kip whispered.

Big Red glanced over his shoulder. "The yeti? He's my cousin."

"What's *his* name?" Daisy asked, fascinated.

"Ha." Big Red snorted. "He keeps trying to get everyone to call him Gandalf the White. Y'know — that wizard from *The Lord of the Rings*? But his real name is Eugene. He's here on a three-week cultural-exchange program with our Himalayan Division. We sent them a skunk ape from Florida in return."

"Holy smokes," Kip murmured. "Bigfoot is *real . . .*"

"Yeah . . . about that . . ." Big Red scratched at his ear, grimacing. "*I* don't mind the nickname, but Eugene's a little sensitive. And prone to occasional fits of irrational rage."

"Right!" Daisy grabbed Kip's arm and pulled him away from the doorway. "Gandalf it is, then."

"Cheers," Big Red nodded with a smile.

"What *is* this place . . . ?"

"The guy who built it calls it the 'Cryptolair.'"

Daisy blinked at him. "The guy who built it?"

"Well, technically it was built with a boatload of government grants, but Dr. Gavin Bafflegab is the, heh, 'mastermind' behind its existence." The sasquatch made the biggest set of air quotes that Daisy had ever seen. "Bafflegab is a cryptozoologist — what those in the scientific community like to refer to as 'an utter crackpot.' And he is. Except he's also *right*."

"The loony fake-monster hunter I told you about, Kildare!" Kip exclaimed.

"Yup." Big Red grinned. "Bet you never thought the loony fake monsters would turn out to be real, eh?"

Kip grimaced. "I didn't mean—"

"It's okay, kid. Just a little monster humour." He chuckled. "Ol' Baffles has been hunting us — collectively we're called 'cryptids' — for decades. Never caught a single one."

"But . . . you're right here!" Daisy was agog. "In his lab! Lair! Thingy!"

The sasquatch grinned mischievously. "I know, right? Only *he* doesn't know that. This is our own little counter-operation. So. You guys wanna have a look around?"

Daisy felt a flutter of excitement in her chest, but when she turned to Kip, she could see worry in his eyes.

She turned back to the sasquatch. "I'm sorry, Big Red," she said. "We're on a rescue mission here. A friend of ours went missing and—"

"Your three-legged marmot pal?" Big Red nodded. "Yeah. We're checking our surveillance footage for the little dude right now."

"Wait. *What?*" Kip blinked up at the sasquatch.

"We got on it as soon as I heard you guys talking about it topside." He shrugged. "We have pretty much the whole forest wired with spy cams and listening devices for our own safety. My guys are going over the digital files from the last few hours. We should know if they have anything soon. In the meantime, let's take that tour!"

CHAPTER 20

BIGFOOTS AND MARMOTS AND RATS — OH MEEP!

"We run the surveillance network from here," Big Red said as he led them on a tour of the facility. "This wing of ol' Doc Bafflegab's complex was mothballed a couple of years ago. Shut down due to a shortage of staffing. I guess it's hard to find good minions these days. Anyway, we snuck in, took over. We tapped into his computer network and now we monitor all of his progress — or, heh, heh, *lack thereof* — from here."

"Holy moly," Kip said. His favourite expression of astonishment had been getting quite a workout over the past few days. "That's . . ."

"Diabolically clever? Yeah, well, *some*body in the Cryptolair had to live up to that expectation." Big Red rolled his eyes and Eugene grunted a knowing laugh.

Daisy was about to ask him what he meant by that when the sasquatch turned and tapped on an observation port that looked out into the deep-blue depths of Lake Okanagan. A few seconds later, a face appeared — a large reptilian face with a longish snout, wide-set dark eyes and shimmering scales.

Daisy yelped an *EEP!* and the face appeared to smile as the creature swam past, flipping an iridescent fin in her direction.

"I was *so* not imagining things when I was a fish!" she said triumphantly to Kip, who was — again — staring, open-mouthed.

"That's Oggy. She's a good egg," Big Red said. "So are her cousins — Iggy, Manny and Winny. They've been here longer than any of us, watching over the water and the wildlife. These days they keep lakeside tourist attractions running across the country and even save the odd careless boater or two when the need arises."

"Wow," Kip murmured. "Holy moly wow."

"C'mon. This way." They followed on the gargantuan heels of the sasquatch as he led them down another low-lit corridor, and exchanged glances of bafflement and wonder as he explained how the cryptids had come to secretly inhabit the disused wing of the Cryptolair.

"It was all Nelson's idea," Big Red continued. "Things were getting a little hot for him back in the old country. He always figured we needed a way to throw some of the more persistent monster hunters off our tails. Then some shady mining company moved into his neck of the woods and started up operations, and he was forced to bug out. I invited him to come hang with me here in beautiful B.C. Together we stumbled across this place and figured we could use the tech to help our fellow cryptids avoid detection."

Daisy wondered who — or what — Nelson was.

"I still can't believe you guys are operating right under the nose of one of the guys who's hunting you!" Kip said, shaking his head and absently propelling himself a metre up the curved wall with a little sideways two-step.

They followed Big Red through another sliding door, into a vaulted chamber humming with equipment. At the centre of a circular bank of computer consoles was a stool that had been raised as high as it would go. On it sat the strangest creature Daisy or Kip had ever laid eyes on. And, considering the last few days, that was saying something! The critter looked like a bunch of different animals combined into one: the body of an over-large hare, pointy fangs, deer antlers, and speckled wings sprouting from its shoulders!

A pair of reading glasses perched on the end of the creature's twitching nose. It was reading a computer screen and occasionally clicking a mouse on the desk in front of it.

"Uh. What's . . . that?" Daisy whispered. "I mean, them. Him? Her . . . ?"

"That's Nelson."

"Right."

"It's not his real name either." Big Red shrugged. "It's just the one we settled on that everyone can pronounce. He's a Pianvian wolpertinger."

"Wolper— wait." Daisy blinked at the sasquatch and exchanged a glance with Kip. "He's *Pianvian*?"

"Yup. Like I said, it was his idea to bring us all together in the first place. See, there's this stuff — it's a rare mineral — called reidium." Big Red raised an eyebrow at Daisy. "*You* might have heard about it. It's found only in certain places in the world—"

"Like Dimly!"

"And Pianvia. There's a whole mountain full of the stuff there."

"Is that what the mining company was after?" Kip asked.

The sasquatch nodded his big hairy head, his expression darkening. "Yeah. Greedy jerks. No respect for the environment."

"Huh." Kip frowned, clearly lost in thought for a moment, and murmured, "I wonder if there's a connection . . ."

"Well," Big Red nodded at the wolpertinger, "we're not exactly sure what the mining operation is all about. Yet. But Nelson here has a theory that all cryptids are, in fact, the result of eons of evolutionary mutations caused by naturally occurring reidium deposits around the world. *It's* incredibly rare. And so are *we*."

Daisy went a bit wide-eyed at the thought. "Does that mean I'm . . . a . . ."

"Oh no. Hey. That's not really what I meant. It's *just* a working theory, Daisy." Big Red gave her a sympathetic glance. "And you're not a cryptid. You're a girl."

"A girl who can do awesome stuff!" Kip chimed in.

"She certainly can," Nelson agreed, jumping down

off his stool and hop-flapping over to them. "And I'd be willing to bet that part of it is because the graphite in that pencil you use was extracted from a source near the reidium mines in Dimly."

Daisy looked down at the odd little creature, her mind churning to catch up with everything she was seeing and hearing. "How did you know—"

"About the pencil? We've been keeping a bit of an eye on you two." He gestured to the bank of monitors, the surveillance equipment Big Red had mentioned. "You see," Nelson continued, "the two substances — graphite and reidium — frequently occur side by side in nature."

"If it's the pencil, why doesn't Kip transmogrify when *he* uses it?" Daisy asked. "He'd at least look like a *normal* something instead of a *weirdo* something."

"My guess," Nelson said, pushing his reading glasses up his forehead so that they nudged against his antlers, "is that *you* were probably exposed to a source of reidium when you were young. But that doesn't alter the fact that Big Red is right. You're not a mutant, nor a cryptid. You're still Daisy Kildare: Normal Girl Who Can Do Awesome Stuff."

Big Red and Kip grinned and high-fived. It almost knocked Kip off his feet. When the sasquatch turned to high-five Daisy, he made sure to be a little gentler.

"Now, Red," Nelson continued, "we're almost done reviewing the files. Why don't you continue with your tour in the meantime?"

They were about to move on to the next room in the complex when Daisy recognized a game Nelson had up on one of his screens. It was *Gang of Greats!* Jess Flem played it obsessively and had tried to teach Daisy some of her secrets. It made Daisy homesick for Dimly. She logged on, hoping to connect with Jess.

Just then a question popped up from Jess's gaming buddy, Gary Lundborg. His gamer name was pretty unforgettable: AsseomeDud27. Gary was, for reasons that were unclear, in need of help translating a phrase from Pianvian into English. Daisy could have just asked Granny Florie but that was a little hard to do from deep inside the Cryptolair. She was a little disappointed she couldn't help Gary out. Or *maybe . . .*

"Hey, Nelson?" she called, remembering the wolpertinger's country of origin. "D'you have any idea what — uh — SPLORG VINU GROZNAB means?"

Nelson did a bunny-hop, then flapped his wings and flew a short distance to land on the desktop near her. "It depends on the context, my dear," he said, pulling his glasses down his twitchy little nose.

Daisy typed a reply to Gary as Nelson explained: "In everyday conversation, it means 'your nana has nice tomatoes.' However, that particular phrase uttered during a fleever match—"

"A what?" Kip asked.

"Fleever," Nelson explained. "It's a sport. The national pastime of Pianvia, the rules of which generally take three days, a chalkboard, a bottle of Splotnik and a PowerPoint presentation to properly explain. In that context, the phrase translates roughly to 'rabid dogs will chew your severed head.'"

"Oh." Kip blinked. "Sounds fun. Bit more intense than, say, soccer."

"Whoa!" Daisy blew a frizzled strand of hair out of her eyes and remembered she still had to ask Jess to erase her self-portrait doodle, but that would have to wait. In the meantime, what on earth did Gary need the Pianvian translation for? Maybe he wanted a fantasy-sounding insult to hurl at other players. She'd have to ask Jess when she got back to regular old civilization.

Or regular old anything, she thought as a sudden flurry of growling, grunting creatures came charging out of a lakeside airlock. Knee high, snaggle-toothed and a pale shade of swampy green, they looked a bit like animated Halloween decorations.

"Are those . . . goblins?" Daisy asked.

"OH!" Big Red made nervous shushing motions

with his hands. "*Shhhh.* Uh. No . . . uh, *shhh!*" He nodded surreptitiously in their direction and said out the side of his mouth, "They're *gremlins.* And they don't like to be confused with *goblins.*"

Another door opened, and an identical pack of rambunctious wee creatures rumbled past.

Daisy waved. "Hello there, grem—"

"WAH!!" Big Red clamped a massive hand over her mouth. "*Those* are goblins."

When they swept past without stopping, Big Red let out a breath of relief. "Yeah, see, you never want to make a gremlin mad. But you NEVER want to make a goblin mad. Gremlins will just pinch you while you sleep. Goblins will delete your bank account."

"Huh," Kip said, frowning faintly. "I thought it would've been the other way around . . ."

"They're *both* pretty fond of Splotnik, though." Big Red rolled his eyes. "I think Nelson regrets introducing them to it."

Screeching like packs of tiny maniacs, the creatures tumbled behind a computer server in a flurry of brawling. A moment later there was a small explosion from behind the piece of equipment and the lights overhead flickered and dimmed for a second.

Eugene the yeti went loping by with a fire extinguisher, sighing, "I'll take care of it . . ."

The Cryptolair tour continued, finally ending high up on a metal catwalk in a huge cavernous room. They overlooked a reservoir full of lake water, with submerged doors that led out to the lake itself and a one-man submersible vehicle docked to one side.

"You know," Big Red said to Daisy as she leaned on the railing, "I'm not sure if I should say anything, but . . . when I was listening in on you two while you were topside? I heard what you said about 'just another useless monster.'"

Daisy was mortified. She hadn't meant to offend anyone. Certainly not anyone as nice as Big Red. "I didn't mean—"

"I know," he said. "I know you didn't mean us. But I've been thinking about it ever since you said it and . . . I guess what I mean is, well, me and the other cryptids? That's kind of what we've been up until now. Useless monsters."

"I don't believe that!"

"Neither do Nelson and Eugene. But Oggy and I have been talking about just what it is we're doing here." His furry brow creased in a frown. "Nessie — y'know, the Loch Ness monster? — well, *she* had a close call a few months back. If the guy hadn't dropped his phone in the water while trying to take a selfie with her, she would've been an internet meme like that!"

He snapped his enormous fingers, setting off a tiny shockwave in the cavernous room. "You see, for years we've been running and hiding, but we can't hide for very much longer. Not if cryptid hunters like Bafflegab and his mystery boss get serious about this business."

"His mystery boss?" Kip asked, exchanging a puzzled glance with Daisy. "What do you mean?"

Big Red shrugged. "We don't know too much about her. Not even what she really looks like. We've only ever intercepted the odd transmission from her base of operations — a blimp."

"*Blimp* . . . ?" Daisy murmured. "I wonder . . ."

"Anyway," Big Red continued, "I was thinking: Instead of all that running and hiding, well, maybe we could be *useful* monsters for once. That's why I had the guys check the recordings. I figure the least we can do is help you guys find your marmot pal. I mean, it's a start, right?"

"You mean *this* 'marmot pal'?" A voice from the reservoir deck called up to them in a snooty, English-accented, mocking singsong. "Come and get it!"

Daisy gasped and Kip made a strangled noise in the back of his throat.

Dr. Gavin Bafflegab was standing there, holding a squirming, struggling Percy by the scruff of his scruffy neck!

"BAFFLEGAB!" Big Red roared.

"GAH!" Bafflegab screamed and almost dropped the marmot. The cryptozoologist's eyes widened to the size of saucers as he stared up at a living, breathing, terrifying specimen of a creature he'd spent his whole life in search of.

"GAH!" he yelped again. "You're . . . you're . . ."

"Real," the sasquatch answered. "Yeah. Real *mad*! Leggo that critter, Doc."

"Ohhhh . . . heeheehehhehhee . . ." Bafflegab started to giggle a bit maniacally. "Oh, I don't think so, my furtive furry friend. GAH!"

Suddenly, the lab door that Daisy was standing in front of slid open with a hiss, and Eugene and Nelson — accompanied by a small horde of goblins and gremlins — burst onto the catwalk.

On the deck, an unhinged grin split Bafflegab's face. "BWAHhahaheeheehee . . . Oh, gracious! Just *look* at you all!" He looked like a six-year-old presented with a pony at a birthday party. A whole *herd* of ponies. "I knew it! I KNEW it!! I've waited my whole life for this— FREEZE!" Bafflegab screeched the command as Big Red and the cryptid crew surged toward the stairs to the deck. "Not another move or I'll drop this beast in the drink!"

He thrust out his arm, dangling Percy over the

water. The marmot yelped pitifully. The cryptids froze as instructed. No one wanted to further endanger Bafflegab's captive. Kip grabbed Daisy's arm, his expression horrified.

"Percy can't swim!" he whispered. "He'll drown! You have to do something! *Draw* something, Daisy!"

Daisy's mind went blank. Just like it had topside. Only . . . *wait!* She glanced around frantically. There were framed posters of cryptids from folk and fairy tales hanging on the walls of the lab leading to the catwalk. While Bafflegab's attention was riveted on the sight of all those real-life cryptids, Daisy skittered into the lab with her pad and pencil, crouched over a desk in front of the first one she saw, and tried to copy it. It might have been cheating but, hey — What was that old saying? Imitation is the sincerest form of flattery? Sure. She'd go with that.

Brow knotted and tongue stuck out, she scribbled away furiously, copying the picture as best she could. What she hadn't really stopped to consider was the actual *subject matter* of the poster: a dragon.

So it came as a bit of a surprise to Daisy when, all of a sudden, she found herself swooping over the catwalk and hovering over the reservoir, belching streams of smoke and flame out of her mouth! And it didn't even sting her throat! That, unfortunately, was her last coherent human thought as her dragon brain took over and her next several thoughts consisted entirely of *BURN!! DESTROY!! BUURRNNNN!!!*

Kip could only stand there blinking at the fiery spectacle. "Uh-oh . . ."

Uh-oh was putting it mildly.

CHAPTER 21

BURN, DAISY, BURN!

A massive flame belched forth from the dragon's muzzle, and everyone in the reservoir room — human and cryptid alike — dove for cover. Everyone except Gerald, who'd snuck onto the catwalk via a back staircase. While their attention was understandably focused on Dragon-Daisy, Gerald kept his considerable wits about him and scurried for Daisy's abandoned art supplies.

Suddenly Gerald's comm device uttered a staticky hiss. He frantically fumbled in his pocket, pulling the thing out to see an image of a plush, rainbow-maned unicorn mask staring at him with empty eyeholes.

"Gerald!" The Boss snapped, clearly annoyed. "I've been trying to reach the Cryptolair for—"

"Can't talk!" Gerald squeaked, stabbing at the *mute* button. "Crucial experiment! Call back later!"

He stuffed the device back into his pocket. Then he nabbed Daisy's sketch pad, pencil and eraser, shoved them into her knapsack, and scampered to safety before anyone noticed, dragging it by one strap with his teeth.

With Dragon-Daisy swooping and diving on mismatched wings, burping fireballs and snorting cinder clouds, most of the cryptids were pinned down, hiding behind whatever cover they could find. The goblins were still mobile, being so little and fast, but the only things they had to hurl at the dragon were insults. Fortunately, that was enough to distract Daisy for a brief instant and she turned her flame breath in their direction. As she did, Big Red leaped into action. He lurched across an open space and hit a big green button on a control console. A deafening alarm sounded as the submerged reservoir doors began to open . . . and Kip saw Oggy the Ogopogo head-butting the steel panels until there was a space between them just big enough for her to squeeze her way into the reservoir, roaring for all she was worth!

Dragons above, sea serpents below. A lesser mad scientist might have given up or made a run for it! But Bafflegab was suddenly in his glory. *This* was his moment to prove himself. Here was his opportunity to capture and command not just the army of cryptids — which The Boss had been hounding him about for*ever* — but the shape-shifting reidium girl to boot!

And because Bafflegab had designed the Cryptolair virtually singlehandedly, he knew all its bells and whistles — and its hidden traps. He fished a remote control out of his lab-coat pocket with the hand not holding a struggling marmot and frantically entered a code sequence. Down in the water, the submersible rumbled to life. Oggy twisted around at the sound but wasn't fast enough to avoid the net that suddenly shot from the sub. It bloomed out and wrapped around her, then pulled tight to trap her hopelessly in a tangle of ropes.

"Gremlin squad!" Nelson shouted. "Put the bite on that net!"

The gremlins dashed for the catwalk railing, flung themselves over, and did cannonballs into the water, where they went to work chewing away at the heavy ropes.

As Kip and Big Red looked on helplessly from above, ducking Daisy's wild fireballs, Gerald suddenly appeared — as if from out of nowhere — hooked a knapsack to an overhead zip line, and sent it whizzing down to the deck.

"Hey, Doc!" Gerald screeched. "Art supplies incoming!"

"NO!" Kip screamed, recognizing the knapsack instantly.

Bafflegab grabbed it, laughed even more maniacally (if that was even possible), and threw the strap over his shoulder. "Now I control the reidium girl! With her, I can control all you monsters! And you—" he said to Percy with a shrug "—have outlived your usefulness!"

Then he hauled back his arm and, with a mighty heave, flung Percy out over the deepest part of the reservoir . . . toward his watery doom.

CHAPTER 22

CRYPTO INFERNO!

It turned out Percy the rescue marmot was aptly named, because in the moment he was cartwheeling helplessly through the air toward a seemingly inevitable *splash-sink-glug-glug* ending, Kip was arrowing down the zip line at superspeed! He reached out, snatched the flailing furball out of mid-air, and tumbled into a perfectly executed tuck-and-roll onto the deck, bouncing up onto the balls of his sneakered feet in a flash.

It *also* turned out the thing with Kip's parkour technique wasn't that he couldn't actually do the moves he thought of, but that he just had to *not* think of them! Stop overthinking. That was the ticket! Kip's downfall (*literally*) had been planning too many moves in advance instead of letting instinct and intuition take over. He hadn't even realized that his moves had vastly improved over the last few days — mostly because he hadn't been aware he was performing them at the time. But in that moment when he reacted without thought to save his pal, Percy was well and truly rescued!

"Yes!" Kip threw a triumphant fist in the air, and Percy squealed with delighted relief. Then together they dove out of the way of one of Dragon-Daisy's random fire belches. "Yikes!"

In the chaos of the moment, Bafflegab scrambled out from behind a storage locker and scurried across the deck toward the submersible.

"Stop right there, you marmot-napping creep!" Kip shouted.

But the cryptozoologist paid him no heed, ducking and dodging until he managed to scamper into the relative safety of the sub. Kip could only watch as Bafflegab pulled the hatch shut behind him and fireballs rained down on the submersible's steel hull. Bafflegab was clearly Daisy's primary target — even her primitive dragon brain recognized him as the biggest, most nefarious threat — but the sub's engines roared to full power and the bulbous little craft was rapidly submerging.

Clouds of steam billowed off the surface of the pool but that was about the extent of the damage. The sub was quickly deep enough that it was unaffected and the underwater doors leading out to the lake were still sliding open ponderously.

In another moment, the gap would be wide enough for Bafflegab to make his escape — and the sea serpent was still trapped in the net! If they didn't do something, Oggy would be dragged into the lake by the sub!

"Chew faster, you guys!" Eugene yelled at the gremlins, who clung to the net, gnawing for all they were worth.

"Curse that remote control!" Nelson squawked from where he was punching away at a computer keyboard. "He's overridden the systems and can control everything with it until we find a way to rejig these security codes!"

The goblins swarmed the control console, but it was hard to see if they were making things better or worse. And overhead, Dragon-Daisy still swooped and dove and — periodically — bumped her head on the walls and ceiling, roaring in outrage.

The sub continued through the water toward the doors.

"We have to keep him here until we can rescue

Oggy!" Big Red shouted. "Or we'll be exposed to the outside world — and then we're all doomed!"

It was true and Kip knew it. If anyone saw the sea serpent, it would be game over for the cryptids. All of them. This was way worse than the Nessie-selfie incident the sasquatch had told them about! Proof of cryptid existence meant their new monster pals would be hunted to extinction all over the world by the likes of Bafflegab.

Kip had to help. Somehow. Risking a scorching, Kip made a run for it. He (expertly!) dodged Dragon-Daisy's blast of breath and, with Percy tucked safely under his arm, bounded up the stairway to the catwalk to see if there was anything he could do.

"Big Red!" he called. "How can I—"

Suddenly Percy leaped from Kip's arms to scrabble across the floor. He disappeared under a work table, and after a few frantic seconds — where all they could hear was squealing and hissing — the homely little marmot came awkwardly trotting back to Kip and the sasquatch, a camouflage-wearing rat dangling from his mouth by his jacket collar.

"Put me down, you varmint!" the rat howled, very much to Kip's surprise.

CHAPTER 23

SWITCHEROO RAT

"I said put me down!" Gerald demanded again. The back of his neck was turning clammy from marmot breath. Percy responded to his demands by vigorously shaking his catch. Tiny pieces of tech equipment flew from Gerald's camo-suit pockets, scattering across the catwalk.

"Well, well, well . . ." the sasquatch said, lumbering over to crouch down in front of Gerald and pegging him with an unblinking stare. "If it isn't Gerald the Wonder Rat. We've been keeping an eye on you. And you better watch who you're calling a varmint, varmint."

"You've got nothing on me, you big galoot." Gerald crossed his arms and stared up at the sasquatch, doing his best to hide his astonishment at the actual existence of such a creature.

"That's Big Red to you, Gerry."

"Let me go."

Big Red and Nelson exchanged a glance.

"Sure. We *could* do that," Nelson said, hopping over. "But with your particular, er, skill set . . . the only gainful employment you're likely to find is in a cage, or back with Bafflegab and The Boss."

Gerald glared at them mutinously and said nothing.

"You're a genetically modified talking rodent," Big Red pointed out. "That . . . Well, come to think of it, *that* pretty much makes you a cryptid, little buddy. Doesn't it, Nelson?"

"Oh yes," the wolpertinger nodded sagely. "Through and through."

"If you stick with the evildoers," Big Red continued, "just how long do you think it'll be before ol' Doc Bafflegab starts to experiment on *you*?"

"I . . . um . . . huh." Gerald blinked his beady little eyes, thinking, *Could it be?* All those years of thinking that he, Gerald, was unique (those ridiculous lab mice simply weren't in his league) and, therefore, all alone in the world— No. Only . . . yes. He'd always — well, ever since he'd developed sentient thought, thanks to the reidium — prided himself on the fact that he was nothing like those mealy mouthed yes-mice Fassbinder lavished all his praise on. Gerald was one of a kind and happy about it.

Except he wasn't. What he was, in fact, was lonely. Kind of like all the other cryptids must have been . . . Until they'd banded together.

"Whaddya say, Gerry?" Kip nudged him. "You feel like putting your genius abilities to work on the side of the good guys?"

If he really *was* a cryptid then he wasn't alone anymore. He sniffed and wiggled his nose. "Only because I don't fancy the idea of becoming a Bafflegab test subject," he grumbled.

Kip and Big Red exchanged a glance.

"Right," Big Red said, nodding. "You're still one bad rat, man. We dig it."

"You bet," said Kip. "Put him down, Percy."

Percy spat Gerald out and sat back on his fat little rump, looking enormously pleased with himself. Kip reached over and gave him a scritch behind his wonky ear.

Gerald brushed the marmot spittle off his collar and tugged the little jacket straight. "Right. What can I do?"

"I don't know." Kip glanced down to where the sub was still straining to gain forward momentum and

Dragon-Daisy was still trying to sear it like a tin-skinned tuna. "All I know is we have to get Daisy's pencil and sketch pad back — before it's too late!"

Gerald trotted over to the table he'd been hiding under and grabbed the strap of another knapsack with his teeth.

"Hey!" Kip said. "What—"

Gerald dragged the bag over to the others and unzipped it, pulling out the contents. "You mean *this* sketch pad and *this* pencil?" he asked, nonchalantly.

"Gerry!" Big Red gaped at him. "Dude!"

"I switched the contents of the packs. Bafflegab

knows the pad and pencil are the keys to that flying spitfire—" Gerald nodded up at Daisy swooping and diving and belching flame "—but I wasn't about to just hand them over to Doc Doofus. He thinks he's so smart? He's got nothing in that bag but a regular old HB pencil painted green and a third-rate rat doodle."

"Gimme!" Kip made grabby hands for the pad. Then he groaned in frustration. "Oh no!" he said. "I don't have—"

"An eraser?"

Kip blinked down at an only slightly smug Gerald, who was clutching a pristine Pink Pearl eraser to his chest.

"You are one seriously genius rat," Kip marvelled.

Gerald handed over the eraser, and Kip went to work carefully obliterating all trace of Daisy's dragon sketch. As he did so, Gerald scurried over to an idle computer terminal and opened up an encrypted email window. He might have turned to the good side, sure, he thought. But that didn't mean he didn't deserve *some* kind of reward from *some*body. Right? While the others were distracted, he scuttled across the keyboard, typing a brief message that began: "Dear Dr. Fassbinder . . ."

CHAPTER 24

DUN-DUN DUN-DUN
DUN-DUN DUN-DUN

"I'm *so* sorry I tried to barbecue you guys!" Daisy wailed, wringing handfuls of Lake Okanagan water out of her crazy hair.

"Never mind that now." Big Red shook his head. "Oggy needs help!"

Kip and the cryptids — and a talking white rat in a camouflage outfit — had fished Daisy out of the reservoir after her detransmogrification and quickly filled her in on the gravity of their present situation.

The submersible was still putt-putting its way out of the reservoir, trailing the sea serpent in the net along with a bunch of still-chewing gremlins. But any second, the little craft would hit open water.

And, well, Daisy *knew* what had to be done.

Without a second thought — or *any* hesitation this time — Daisy lunged for her pencil and cast her mind back to the goldfish sketch she'd tried to draw with the normal HB pencil. And then she thought about the fish she'd successfully sketchied up by the lake. And then, well, practice made perfect, right? That's what Kip kept telling her. Third time's the charm, right? That's what she told herself. So she took *another* stab at drawing a fishy shape. Only this time it wasn't *quite* a goldfish.

It wasn't even the unidentifiable second fish. This time, it was a Great. White. Shark.

Sure — it was the *ugliest* great white shark that had ever flipped a dorsal fin, but who cares?! None of the sharks she'd seen on Shark Week would ever win a beauty pageant either. She finished the sketch, felt the *tingle-snap* lightning strike of the reidium activation, heard the theme from the movie *Jaws* in her head, and flung the sketch pad like a Frisbee in Kip's direction, yelling, "Kip! Catch!"

As she felt herself transmogrifying and falling into the waters of the Ogo-tank, Daisy saw Kip sailing through the air to catch the sketch pad in a *perfectly* executed parkour jump — with bonus backflip!

She cheered, but it sounded more like "YRARRR-RGH!" Her massive shark jaws snapped and threshed, full of snaggled shark teeth that could turn a submersible into a tin can. A tin can full of holes! First thing she did was accomplish with one bite what the gremlins had been trying unsuccessfully to accomplish with many — she chomped through the tether that held the net to the submersible. It was like biting through a licorice rope — a fresh one, not the tough stale ones that had been lying around on the counter after she'd forgotten to close the package — and within seconds, Oggy was swimming free! The gremlins did little underwater dances of gremlin joy and rushed to their cryptid buddy.

Shark-Daisy roared a triumphant burst of bubbles. Then she turned her attention to the sub. Her shark brain registered that Nelson must have finally figured out how to block Bafflegab's remote-control commands, because the underwater reservoir doors had reversed direction and were slowly closing. Soon Bafflegab would have nowhere to run—

FWOOOOSH! Shark-Daisy recoiled in surprise as the sub's escape pod shot past her nose, through the narrow gap left between the doors and into the lake beyond. Lake Okanagan was 135 kilometres long.

They weren't going to catch him. Not this time.

CHAPTER 25

CRYPTO-VICTORIOUS

"He'll be back," Nelson said, as Daisy dried off with a monogrammed Cryptolair towel. "And we'll be ready for him. Thanks to you two."

"Yeah," Big Red said. "We owe you guys."

"Heck, no you don't!" Kip said. "Without you, who knows what would have happened to Percy."

They all looked over at Percy curled up on the knapsack, asleep and blissfully snoring. Curled up right beside him, Gerald the extraordinary lab rat was snoring too.

"He's got potential," Daisy said with a grin. "I think you guys will make a great team, you know?"

Big Red nodded, a smile crossing his broad, hairy face. "I think you're right."

Meanwhile, high up on the catwalk, no one even noticed the tiny comm device still broadcasting a signal from the Cryptolair. The screen displayed the muted image of a rainbow-maned unicorn head . . . with empty eyeholes that still somehow managed to convey . . . an expression . . . of *astonishment* . . .

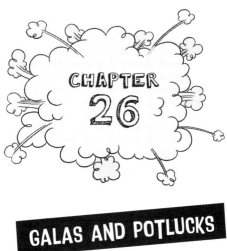

CHAPTER 26

GALAS AND POTLUCKS

The photo collage Daisy and Kip managed to cobble together in the final few hours of their last day of Art Camp — a series of grainy, out-of-focus and generally (intentionally) confusing pictures of the cryptid gang, interspersed with a few of Daisy's hastily rendered *non*-Dimly-pencil sketches and highlighted by some truly astonishing photos that Kip had snapped of Daisy in her various sketchy states — got RAVE reviews from the Artists' Council at the barbecue gala.

Kip told Daisy in an amused whisper that it was probably because the whole thing was so *un*artistic that everyone was afraid to say so, in case they were the one missing something.

So, with many tilted heads and eye squints and "hmmmms" and "aaah . . . yeeess'es," the exhibit was pronounced a roaring success full of "social relevance" and "environmental activism," with a "healthy and robust disregard for conventional rules in service of a greater good."

Kind of like Daisy, Kip and their new set of impossible friends, really.

The accolades stopped short of an invitation to exhibit in a New York gallery, but there was an invitation of another kind waiting for Daisy a week after school started back.

When she opened up her locker that following Monday, a dingy grey envelope, frayed at the corners from many uses and stained with coffee-cup rings, fell out.

Daisy gingerly opened it and pulled out a sheet of paper that had an old budget spreadsheet from 1998 printed on one side and a message to her — in faint, fading end-of-the-toner-cartridge printing — on the other. Some of the printed words were crossed out, with handwriting above.

"What are you reading?" Kip asked, walking toward her.

And then he blinked, a startled expression crossing his face.

"What?" Daisy asked.

"Uh . . . nothing . . . did you get a new hairdo in the last few minutes?"

"*What?*" Daisy put a hand to her hair. It was soft and manageable!

She could feel her usual waves falling around her shoulders, not the frizzed-out corkscrew tangles she'd been sporting for so many days she had *almost* gotten used to them!

"Yes!" she exclaimed. "Way to go, Jess!"

The birthday card with its Daisy doodle must have been destroyed somehow. And she couldn't have been happier.

For a moment, she thought she could smell something kinda . . . bad. Like, monster-bad-breath bad . . . *Heh. Maybe something horrible ate the card*, she thought. Like an actual monster.

And then she decided she didn't want to know. If Jess Flem was having any kind of month even *close* to hers, Daisy could wait to find out. So she just shrugged.

"So . . . what are you reading?" Kip asked again, leaning in to peer over her shoulder.

"I'm . . . not sure," Daisy said, and held the thing out for him to see.

It read:

Daisy Kildare
YOU'RE INVITED! are alive and we found you!
If you're reading this you ~~survived your mission.~~
^
Congratulations!
To celebrate a year of (mostly) successful projects, come to our midsummer potluck picnic for those still alive.
Let us know if you'll bring salad, sandwiches or dessert. (And also cheese.)
Looking forward to seeing whoever is left.

Bernard Cheeper,
Department C Projects Coordination

PS You can bring one guest.

"Who's Bernard Cheeper?" Kip asked.

"I have no idea." Daisy shook her head, mystified. "Guess I'll find out, right?"

"You're not seriously thinking of accepting a mysterious invitation to some random clearly-a-trap potluck, are you?" Kip lowered his voice, glancing up and down the mostly empty hallway. "When we both know there are real, actual nefarious supervillains in the world?"

"Well, no," Daisy said with a shrug. "Of course not. At least, I'm not going to go alone." Then she turned

"Actually, Archie, you are below normal." The doctor pulls at his moustache. He's got a beauty, curled up around his nose.

"I must be *extra*-qualified for your study then, eh?" Archie starts to laugh some more but gets distracted by his hands. He turns them into giant crab claws.

"Hah! Take that!" He attacks the doctor's arm with his claws. *Snap, snap, snap.*

The doctor sighs. "Two more questions, Archie. Have you noticed anyone paying attention to you? Following you around?"

"Eh?" says Archie. He says this a lot.

"How about a hot-air balloon? Have you ever looked up and seen one of those, closer than it should be?"

"A blimp?"

scary music (Yup. There it is.)

"Like at a baseball game? Following me? I dunno. How would I notice? I don't spend my time looking up."

"Why indeed." The doctor sighs again. "All right. Last question. You are thirteen years old now. Puberty is a time of great change. Have you noticed any gifts that today's tests might not be able to pick up?"

"You mean, can I fly or turn invisible? Or shoot lasers from my eyes? Or tell what someone else is thinking? Ho, ho, ho. Let's check. What are you thinking, Doc? Wait! Don't move. I'm getting a signal . . ."

BORED MUCH?

ack at the Boredom Institute, Archie has almost finished this year's tests. He's written a logic quiz, had his reflexes checked, lifted weights, run on a treadmill, held his breath. Now he's putting his shirt back on.

"Hoawmmmm," says Dr. Fassbinder, checking the screens. "Below average in everything again. But don't feel bad, Archie."

"*Me,* feel bad?" says Archie. "You're the one running these stupid tests. Call these tests? Your whole set-up's a joke. That kid with the runny nose. Jess? If she's gifted, I'm an aardvark. And Daisy. She comes here too, right? What's with her? At least I'm normal."

**FOUR BOOKS.
FOUR AUTHORS.
FOUR UNFORGETTABLE
SUPERHEROES.**

Super Sketchy by Lesley Livingston
Hey, look, you're holding it in your hand!

Mucus Mayhem by Kevin Sylvester, available now
Jessica Flem is allergic to everything except video games.
She's used to a nose that never stops running, but is not
prepared for the mysterious power that shows up around
her thirteenth birthday. Could there be a use for all those
snot-filled tissues? She's about to find out . . .

What Blows Up by Ted Staunton, available now
Gary "Clumsborg" Lundborg is more than a little surprised
to suddenly find himself moving objects with his mind
— not gracefully, often distractedly, and only between
three and six in the morning. Will this help him become a
basketball star? Well, first he must save the world . . .

Irresistible by Richard Scrimger, available October 2019
Archie O'Kaye mostly rubs people the wrong way.
But when he becomes utterly charming right before
everyone's eyes at his thirteenth birthday party, his family
and friends know something is up. And they're not the
only ones watching . . .

Visit www.scholastic.ca/almost-epic
for chapter excerpts, videos and more!

pointed in the right directions, but they've managed an absolutely heroic job of doing just that! All while being a joy, a pleasure and an inspiration to work with. Eternal gratitude to you both (and maybe a bottle of Aspirin).

Superpowered fist bumps also go out to my personal cadre, especially wonder-agent Jessica Regel, who didn't even blink or question my sanity (that much) when I told her about this project. Jonathan Llyr, of course, did question my sanity. But that's just, like, a normal Tuesday.

But the most heroic high-fives go out to the readers, and to the squads of teachers, librarians and booksellers who get the books into all those grabby hands. You guys truly are EPIC. No ifs, ands or almosts about it.

LESLEY LIVINGSTON is an award-winning author of teen fiction best known for her Wondrous Strange trilogy and Valiant series. She is the co-author, with Jonathan Llyr, of the middle-grade series The Wiggins Weird. Prior to her writing life, Lesley was a principal performer in a Shakespearean theatre company. Lesley's personal superpower is an inadvertent ability to manipulate the timestream to reliably get her anywhere thirteen minutes AFTER her target time.

Acknowledgements

The act of writing is not, as it is popularly portrayed in film and television, a solitary act performed by a deep-thinking soul wandering the moors, or sitting in a shabbily romantic garret, or haunting a café with a notebook and fountain pen . . . Wait. What? It *is*? Ah. Well. I've been dong this wrong then.

In this case, I must thank/blame the magnificent weirdos I've enjoyed the giddy pleasure of conspiring with to help bring the story of our quirky Dimly quartet to life. Scrimger was the first of these crazed creatives — the one who tapped me on the shoulder and, with a maniacal gleam in his eye, said, "Hey! Wanna do this bonkers thing?" But it was Staunton and Sylvester who assured me that, no, no, it was a perfectly normal thing and not at all bonkers. They were, of course, wrong. Just ask Britt! Group superhug, guys. You four are the best.

Seriously, though, working on this series has indeed been bonkers. But in the best possible way. Just ask our long-suffering Supertastic Scholastic crew — chief among them the Amazing Anne Shone and the Extraordinary Erin Haggett, who must have been professional feral cat herders in another life. I swear. We are not the easiest bunch to round up and get

to him and grinned, pointed at the word 'guest,' and said, "Whoever these guys in Department C are? They spelled best-ever superhero sidekick wrong."

Kip couldn't help but smile. "I guess we're in this together. You bringing the fruit salad?"

Archie puts his finger to his forehead and closes his eyes. "Hey. Maybe I do have a gift, Doc. I know what you're thinking right now: *Wow, that Archie O'Kaye is a real dork. I never want to see him again!*"

Dr. Fassbinder almost smiles. "Are you sure you don't have telepathic powers? That was very close."

"Doc," says Archie, "if I could turn myself invisible, I'd be robbing a candy store. Or pranking Big Mean Ehsin. I'd sneak up behind him and tie his shoelaces together. Yeah! That's what I'd be doing if I had a superpower."

"Yeasss, you probably would," says the doctor, making a note on a file. It reads: *A. O'Kaye. No talent. Self-absorbed. Unformed personality — like a baby. Most unlikeable child I ever met. Do not schedule for next year. Never wish to see him again.*

"I guess we are done here," says Dr. Fassbinder. "I don't know what we will decide to do next year. Perhaaaaps—" He breaks off when Archie screams.

"Eek!" Archie stands on his chair, pointing down at the floor. One, two, four furry little creatures have dashed out from under the doctor's desk. "Mice!" Archie shrieks. "I can't stand mice! I— I—"

The doctor chuckles. "Don't be afraid, Archie. These are my assistants: Marvin, Denise, Elaine, Claude."

The mice wear lab coats. Two carry clipboards. The one in spectacles — Claude — waves a teeny paw.

The doctor explains. "These mice were exposed to reidium. Look what it's done to them. They are almost a different species — supermice. I've been interested in you, Gary, Daisy and Jessica ever since *your* reidium exposure. Daisy and Jessica are progressing in very interesting ways. I don't know about Gary yet — I see him in a few minutes. But in your case, Archie, I just can't locate any kind of super—"

He breaks off abruptly. And stares at Archie as he climbs down from his chair. The boy's hair is neater. Somehow, his shirt is tucked in. His smile is as white and magnetic as the North Pole.

"Hi . . . I mean, hello there. How . . . totally *wonderful* to meet you all," Archie says to the mice, bending low.

There is a collective high-pitched gasp. Dr. Fassbinder rises to his feet. "You . . ." he begins.

"No, no, it's *you*, Doctor." Archie faces him. "I simply can't thank you *enough* for . . . all you've done. I'm just terribly sorry I seem to have let you down."

"No, no, no. Not at all, Archie. We've enjoyed every second of your wonderful visit." Dr. Fassbinder shakes his head to clear it. He checks his onscreen file notes, which now read: *A. O'Kaye. Amazing potential. Could do anything. Most likeable child I ever met. Must see again next year. Reminder to Dept C to book him first-class tickets. Check his hotel status.*